KING BLOOD

'The toughest crime novels ever . . . Thompson's fans claim he wrote better books than Hammett did and Chandler. The claim is fatuous; he didn't write their kind of story at all. The first thing to be said about Thompson is that his fiction resembles no one else's. The distinguishing marks of his novels are a high degree of death, a varying degree of comedy, some astonishing play with psychology, and most important – the absence of any moral centre at all. Hammett, Chandler and Macdonald, the so-called hard-boiled writers, were crusading moralists: cynical though their private eyes may be, they restore moral order to their twilight worlds. In Thompson's novels, morality is replaced by ambition. His protagonists are incompetent, usually psychotic, carnivores; like the people they kill, they're losers – they just leave more of a mess before they go'
Peter S. Prescott, *Newsweek*

'Jim Thompson was the king . . . Thompson's vision makes him like nobody else. His is a world peopled with psychopathic killers, expensive sluts, crooked cops, moronic publishers, filthy-minded doctors, cretins, perverts, obsessives . . . Thompson's novels don't have good guys, just anti-heroes and the women who deserve them'
Roderick Thorp

'Jim Thompson had more pistolero savvy than all the so-called *great* American writers . . . Thompson was a hammer to their feather dusters'
Harlan Ellison

'The master of the anti-hero, tough-guy genre'
Publishers Weekly

'Thompson's writing is dense, lurid, idiomatic, musical in its speech rhythms . . . full of weird detours . . . alternatively plaintive and obscene . . . raucous . . . and bitterly funny'
Geoffrey O'Brien, *Village Voice*

James Myers Thompson was born in Oklahoma in 1906. As well as working on an oil pipeline in Texas, as a steeplejack, burlesque actor, professional gambler and seller of bootleg whisky, Thompson wrote for several newspapers, including the *New York Daily News* and *Los Angeles Times Mirror*. During this time he wrote no less than twenty-nine novels, many of which have been made into films in America and France: most notably *The Getaway*, filmed by Sam Peckinpah, starring Steve McQueen; *Pop. 1280*, filmed as *Coup de Torchon*, by Bertrand Tavernier; *The Killer Inside Me*, by Burt Kennedy, starring Stacy Keach; and *A Hell of a Woman*, filmed as *Serie Noire*, by Alain Corneau. He also wrote the screenplays for Stanley Kubrick's *The Killing* and *Paths of Glory*. The last few years of Thompson's life were marred by alcoholism and are chronicled in two works, *The Alcoholics* and *Bad Boy*. When he died at the age of 71, on 7th April 1977, not one of his novels was available in his native America and his reputation had reached its lowest ebb. However, critical opinion of his novels has grown steadily in the intervening years, and Jim Thompson has finally been reinstated amongst the greats like Raymond Chandler, Horace McCoy and Dashiell Hammett.

Also by Jim Thompson

RECOIL
A HELL OF A WOMAN
SAVAGE NIGHT
THE KILL-OFF
WILD TOWN
THE GETAWAY

and published by Corgi Books

KING BLOOD

Jim Thompson

CORGI BOOKS

KING BLOOD
A CORGI BOOK   0 552 13241 1

Originally published in Great Britain by
Sphere Books Ltd.

PRINTING HISTORY
Sphere edition published 1973
Corgi edition published 1989

This book is set in 11/12pt. Plantin by
County Typesetters, Margate, Kent

Corgi Books are published by Transworld Publishers Ltd.,
61–63 Uxbridge Road, Ealing, London W5 5SA, in Australia
by Transworld Publishers (Australia) Pty. Ltd., 15–23 Helles
Avenue, Moorebank, NSW 2170, and in New Zealand by
Transworld Publishers (N.Z.) Ltd., Cnr. Moselle and
Waipareira Avenues, Henderson, Auckland.

Made and printed in Great Britain by
Cox & Wyman Ltd., Reading, Berks

CHAPTER ONE

a

Just before first-light, just before dawn began its streaky buttering of the Territorial Oklahoma prairie, Critch stepped out to the open vestibule of the train and stood waiting there for the soldier's bride. She had to stop by the toilet (small wonder!) before she could join him, so there was time to brace himself for what he would do if her attitude demanded it; to visualize the ultimate scene in a drama of robbery and rape.

Let the little lady get troublesome, and he'd knock her off the platform. Send her down between the two cars, and the grinding wheels of the train. There were seven cars behind this one. By the time they were done with her, the little lady would be mincemeat. A nothingness which would be less than nothing when daybreak brought coyotes and buzzards.

Chuckling softly, Critch lighted a cheroot, thinking how praiseful Ray would have been had he been alive to praise. Oh, Ray would have approved handsomely. With, perhaps, one minor reservation.

Your eye on the target, dear boy. The vital spot. Which, I may add, is never found in the uterus. Unless — ha, ha — you're much better equipped than I.

Ah, Ray, Ray! But there were exceptions to all rules; and sometimes a pupil outstrips his teacher.

The money was under her clothes, so how else could he get at it, except through the guise of love? And getting the money where he had gotten it had been his insurance. Unless she were a fool, she couldn't talk now. Unless a fool, she wouldn't try to retaliate. Otherwise, and regardless of her innocence in her despoiling, she would have to explain what could never be explained. Not to a husband. Not to any man who would be her husband. Not in this day and age.

Critch puffed at his cheroot, meditating with unaccustomed wistfulness on Ray, the man who had been his guide and guardian for so many years. It was hard to think of Ray as having gotten old, of losing any of the craftiness which had pulled him out of so many tight places. Yet, despite the youthfully dapper body and the incredibly young face, he *had* aged. Ray had gotten old, and his age showed in his tendency to waver when decisiveness was imperative, his quibbling and pettiness, and an incipiently fatal furtiveness of eye and manner.

As Critch saw it, there was only one thing to be done. That which Ray would have done had their situations been reversed. Having done it, survival required that he put distance between himself and the victim of his betrayal. He put it there, brushing out his tracks as he fled.

Ray remained in Texas. Critch wound up in the distant Dakotas. So, happily, he had not been present at the end, and could only witness it vicariously via a newspaper artist's eyes.

Critch sincerely hoped that either the eyes or the artist had been bad. It would have pained him – for a little while at least – to believe that Ray's handsome neck had been stretched the length of his body.

6

(Critch tossed away his cheroot, impatiently. What the hell was keeping her? Had the damned fool fallen in the toilet?)

b

Tulsa lochopocas. A clanning place of the Osages.

It stood at the twin-forks of the Arkansas, near the confluence of the Verdigris; a center of commerce (in so far as there was any) and a conference site long before white man ever set foot on the American continent.

Tulsa lochopocas. Tulsey town. Tulsa.

Critch had liked the looks of it from the moment he stepped off the train from Kansas City. It was a higgledy-piggledy kind of place, with streets running casually whatever way they damned pleased, and buildings sprawling and crawling all over hell and back in the ages-old pattern of quick money.

It was his kind of town, he had thought. An easy-money town. A railroad and river town, a cotton and cattle town. Furs, lumber, foodstuffs. All flowed into and through Tulsa, an endless stream of increment. And now there was even oil, for prospectors with a spring-pole rig had drilled through the red-clay soil to a respectable gusher. In these surroundings, and without refining facilities, it had little commercial value as yet, being almost as worthless as some of those minerals you heard about only in books; uranium, for example. But never mind. There was plenty of money without oil, and the place virtually shouted the news that here one could do whatever he was big enough to do.

Thus, Critch saw Tulsa. Correctly, he saw it so. What he did not see was something indefinable,

7

something that far wiser and better men had failed to see at first glimpse of Tulsa (Tulsey Town, *tulsa lochopocas*). Men who nominally *were* big enough to do whatever they attempted.

Approximately two centuries before, a man named Auguste Choteau led a small army of his countrymen up the Arkansas, professional hunters and trappers who had followed him profitably and safely all the way from France; and they had tied up their longboats here at the twin-forks of the river – so patently perfect it was for their ends – and they had gone about their business of getting rich quickly.

They were not hoggish about it. Not for a moment would they have enriched themselves while impoverishing the Indians. It had always been French policy to make friends with the Indians, and Choteau, a good man and a gentleman, would have done so anyway. He and his men intended to found a permanent settlement here; had even gone so far as to pick a name for it, the name of their patron saint. They would build a city here, one in which French and Osage would be equal. And how, why, being reasonable men, and to make these great events possible, could the Osages object to the sharing of a fraction of their furry wealth when they had such an unusable abundance of it?

The Osages confessed to being reasonable men. Being reasonable, they suggested that there was no valid reason for sharing what they already owned, and that it was their prerogative, not the Frenchmen's, to decide whether or not they needed it all.

The Choteau party became irritated. They got very firm with the denizens of *tulsa lochopocas*. Nor were they the last to do so. For Tulsey Town's bland independence, her notion that she should deal with the world strictly on *her* terms, grew stronger each day of her rambunctious history.

More than two hundred years after her off-handed brushing-off of the French trappers and hunters, Tulsa was telling Wall Street to take its underwriting and financing and get hence (or words to that effect). The House of Morgan, *et al*, were amused rather than annoyed. The notion that an upstart Oklahoma town could itself raise the billions necessary for the proper exploitation of its oil resources was simply laughable. And yet . . . the upstart town *did* raise those billions. Not only for itself but for others. And in the end, Wall Street was forced to admit that it had a rival. It remained first, in the big money capitals of the world, as a financier of the oil industry. But little Tulsa – or, rather, not-so-little Tulsa – ranked second to it.

So there you were, then. There Tulsa was. A friendly town, an amiable live-and-let live town. A proud town, which liked doing things its own way and knew just what to do with those who would have it otherwise.

As late as the early years of the Twentieth Century, there was riverboat traffic as far north as the Dakotas. So relatively much, compared with railroad commerce, that the midwest was visualized as the future population center of the country, and there was agitation to move the nation's capital from its eastern site to some more suitable spot in Nebraska Territory.

Because of her location, Tulsa was host to no small number of riverboat travelers, and she provided for them characteristically. Graves, for some. Tar and feathers for others. For others – those whose notions coincided with her own – homes and happiness, and often wealth.

Similarly, when the Cherokee Strip was thrown open to settlement and the great ranches broken up into quarter-section homesteads, Tulsa provided for the now-jobless cowboys, the adventurers and desperadoes who had formerly roamed the Strip; taking care of them – in one way or another. And when the homesteaders, often underfinanced, were drouthed out or otherwise brought to disaster in their first season, Tulsa was again a provider – in her own fashion.

Tulsa knew just what to do about the Crazy Snake rebellion, the last of the Indian uprisings. She knew just what to do – and she did it – when race riots threatened to destroy the city. She . . .

But that is getting ahead of the story. Moving back a couple of hundred years to Auguste Choteau and his men:

Their 'firmness' with the residents of *tulsa lochopocas* was repaid with interest. The Frenchmen were, in fact, forced to flee for their lives; heading their long boats on up the Arkansas, and thence into and up the Mississippi, along whose shores, in an uninviting stretch of mudflats, they at last established their permanent settlement, duly naming it after their patron saint.

It became a large and prosperous city, even as they had predicted. A city which Critch had often visited to his advantage. Now, at the end of his second day in Tulsa, with his wallet empty and the place where he carried it sore from a Tulsan's kicking, Critch cursed the foolish fate that had guided him here instead of to the friendly metropolis of Auguste

Choteau's founding, the city of St. Louis.

In fact, Tulsa had so unnerved him that he was even fearful of responding to the small box-notice in the local newspaper. A boldface-type announcement that Critchfield King, youngest son of Isaac Joshua King, should immediately present himself at the offices of Judge Washington Dying Horse, attorney-at-law.

c

It took a night of hunger and sleeplessness, a very long night without money for food or room, to change his fearfulness to fatalism and the conclusion that life could dip him in no sourer pickle than he was already in. In the morning, then, after shaving and tidying up at the railroad station, he at last presented himself at Judge Dying Horse's office.

They faced each other across the attorney's deal desk. Critch smiling equably, his manicured hands resting on the fake-gold head of his cane; the lawyer studying him out of dark and deep-set eyes, his bronzed face expressionless. Critch knew this waiting technique. The simple trick of it was to *wait*, forcing one's opponent – and the world was made up of opponents – to tip his hand.

At last the deep-set eyes surrendered to a blink, and their owner spoke. 'So you're Critchfield King, and you're twenty-three years old.'

'I am and I am,' Critch smiled, 'and you're Judge Washington, uh – I don't believe I've encountered the name before, sir? Cherokee, isn't it?'

It was gross flattery; the Cherokees were highly cultured, the most advanced of the Five Civilized Tribes. The attorney flatly rejected the compliment.

11

'The judge is honorary, Mr. King, and the name is Osage. One of the *un*-civilized tribes. *Uncivilizable* in the opinion of the United States government. That's why we were allocated this particular area of Oklahoma, one that ostensibly was only good for fishing and hunting rather than farming.'

'So?' Critch made subtle alterations in his smile. 'So you're plain Mr. Dying Horse, Osage lawyer, and you wanted to see me, Critchfield King, youngest son of Isaac Joshua King. Why?'

'I want you,' frowned the Osage, 'to tell me about yourself from the time you fled your father's bed and board with your mother and her lover—'

'I didn't flee it,' Critch lied. 'They abducted me.'

'That's likely; you were only ten. Now tell me all about yourself – what you've done, what you've become – from the age of ten to the present.'

'Why?'

'Why not?'

'Because there isn't much good to tell. Suppose you had been dominated by a professional criminal and a mother who was a whore and worse for the better part of your life. How much would you have to be proud of?'

'Well . . .' Attorney Dying Horse nodded grudgingly. 'But your mother herself ran away from this man. Chance – Raymond Chance – after a few years.'

'She did. Which left me completely under his control.'

'Didn't it occur to you to run away also?'

'It did, and I did.' Another lie, but it had all the earmarks of truth. 'Unfortunately, I didn't have my mother's, uh, resources for survival. It wasn't until a few years ago that I was finally able to make it.'

'Mmm. And since then?'

12

'A number of things. Bartender. Steamboat steward. Hotel clerk. Salesman . . .' The truth here; half the truth. He had had all those occupations, and many more, but only as springboards, entrees, to devious enterprise. 'I've spent most of my time lately in speculation.'

'Cotton?'

'What else?'

Dying Horse gave him a slow totting up: the expensive suit and hat; the handmade boots and spotless linen. A fine-looking, well-spoken young man. One who was almost too handsome; too plausible. Indian instinct whispered that here was a man neither to be liked nor trusted, yet he did like him and he did trust him.

'You seem to have done well at speculating, Mr. King.'

'I've made a living.'

'Such transactions are hard to trace.'

'Impossible, I'd say.'

'In fact,' the attorney persisted doggedly, 'I doubt that any part of your story could be checked on for truth and veracity.'

'I doubt it, too. And?'

The Osage sighed; laughed a little irritably. Instinct gave way to the compelling charm and personality of Critch King's (when he cared to use it), and abruptly he slammed his desk with an emphatic bronzed hand.

'And, Mr. King,' he said, coming to his feet, 'I think we should continue this discussion over drinks.'

In the private room of one of Tulsa's fancier saloons, an establishment with carpeted floors and crystal chandeliers, the lawyer poured whiskey for them and held a match to Critch King's cigar. He took a delicate taste of the liquor, studying his young guest over the brim of his glass. Critch was interestedly examining a framed document which hung on the wall – a handwritten testimonial to the saloon, signed by Washington Irving.

'You know *A Tour of the Prairies*, Mr. King?'

'I thought I did until I saw this.' Critch nodded at the document. 'I didn't know Mr. Irving was ever in the Tulsa area.'

Dying Horse chuckled approvingly; agreed that the point was certainly moot. 'But we've had the printing arts, and the arts and craftsmen associated with them, in Eastern Oklahoma for a very long time. George Creekmore's newspaper was possibly the first major periodical west of the Mississippi.'

'A Cherokee language newspaper,' Critch nodded. 'Then this testimonial is probably a forgery?'

'Mmm. Done by a tramp journeyman with a small talent and a large thirst. Like the etching over there, for example.'

Critch arose and walked over to the far wall. He took a long look at the drawing which hung there, a picture of an Indian mounted on a pony, their heads bowed dispiritedly as they stared down the face of a cliff.

'No' – With a shake of his head, Critch sat back down at their table. 'I'd have to disagree with you there, sir. That's a genuine Remington if I ever saw one.'

'You're a good judge of art, Mr. King!'

'Thank you, sir.'

'You're a remarkable young man, all around. How anyone could have overcome the handicaps you must have suffered to become a gentleman and a scholar . . . !'

Critch murmured appreciation for the lawyer's good opinion, modestly pointing out that hardship often brought out the best in a man. 'When a man's got no one to help him, he simply has to try harder. At least, that's the way I've always seen it. If a man truly wants to make something of himself, he can do it, regardless of birth and background!'

Dying Horse looked into his guest's innocently earnest young face, his heart warming as it seldom did to a white man. *Regardless of birth.* Now here was understanding for you! Here was a man who knew what it was to suffer and struggle against unbearable odds.

God damn Ike King! he thought. Practically on his death-bed, and he treats his own son like this!

He took a quick drink, then another. Critch smiled at him gently, gave one of the bronzed hands a comforting pat.

'Don't let it upset you, Judge. I haven't seen my father since I was a child, but I don't imagine he's changed any.'

'No.'

'I've often thought that if he'd treated my mother a little differently . . .' Critch shook his head regretfully. 'She was part Creek, you know, and she had rather crisp, curly hair. Dad used to accuse her of being part Negro.'

'He did, eh?' Dying Horse laughed angrily. 'Sounds about like him!'

'Of course, there was some intermarriage among the Creeks,' Critch shrugged. 'But what of it, anyway? At any rate, why taunt a woman publicly

15

with something she couldn't help?'

The Osage gulped another large drink, a red flush spreading under the lighter hue of his face. He brought the heavy glass down on the table with a bang.

Getting a little drunk, Critch thought shrewdly. When will these stinking Indians learn that they can't drink?

'Mr. King – *hic, hup* – your father is, as you may know, my client in this area. It was my duty, if you could be found, to look you over and to decide whether you were fit to be claimed as his son and heir. I have decided, in the affirmative. The only question in my mind is whether he is fit to be claimed as your father!'

Critch smiled a soft demurral. After all, they shouldn't be too hard on the old man.

'I'll welcome the chance to see him before he dies. I would have gone back before this, but I wasn't sure of my reception.'

'You'll find it satisfactory,' Dying Horse assured him, 'under the circumtances. Now, if you were down on your luck, if you'd been a failure in life and really needed help . . .'

'I'd certainly never go near Dad,' Critch laughed, ruefully. 'A strange man, my father, but fair – absolutely fair – in his own way. He never excused his own failures, so why should he excuse them in others?'

'But his own son,' the lawyer protested. 'His own flesh and blood!'

'Only if he chose to claim me as a son,' Critch pointed out. 'Which he wouldn't do unless I met his standards.'

They talked a while longer. Then, the lawyer glanced at the clock and remembered an appointment. As he reached for his wallet and beckoned to a waiter, Critch laid a ten-dollar bill on the table.

'My treat, Counsellor. I insist.'

'Nonsense. Business, Mr. King, so we're both the guests of your father. I—' he broke off scowling, slapping his hip. 'God damn it!' he said. 'I've lost my wallet!'

'Why, that's too bad,' Critch frowned sympathetically. 'Was there very much in it?'

'Well, not a great deal. Fifty dollars or so.'

God damn! thought Critch.

He lingered over his drink while the attorney hastened away to his appointment. Then, after a leisurely free lunch provided by the establishment, he visited the backyard privvy where he emptied the wallet of money and dropped it down the hole.

Out on the street again, he sauntered through the mid-day throngs, his expression suave and smiling, his eyes alert for yet another wink from fortune. For certainly it would not be smart to present himself to Ike King with such picayune pickings as he had now. There was his ticket to buy, and his meals and incidental expenses. He would be virtually broke on arrival, a very dangerous way to be with a sire like old Ike. Isaac Joshua King might well haul out a fatted calf for the returning prodigal, a figuratively golden calf, but only if the returnee was herding a few steers in front of him as proof of his merit.

The relatively few dollars stolen from Attorney Dying Horse represented nothing more than another chance. It was something to build on, something to be used in trimming a truly well-heeled sucker.

CHAPTER TWO

a

Raymond Chance had come to King's Junction in the guise of a capitalist, a man seeking likely land in which to invest his money. He was a very plausible and personable man, needless to say, and he was equipped with a number of impressive letters of introduction, all fakes, of course, like his handsomely engraved sheaf of cashier checks. As a guest of the Junction Hotel, which was also the King ranch-house, he had ready access to Isaac Joshua who was not unagreeable to selling some of his own land, providing the price was right.

Ike had better things to do, by his own admission, than to drive prospective purchasers over his holdings. Nor was it necessary for him to do so, since his woman could do it just as well, and, like all women, never did nothin' much useful anyways that he could see. Neither could he see (he joked jovially) that he was doing anything chancy in having his wife traipse around all day with such a good-lookin' young feller, because anyone that wanted a half-nigger Creek was sure as hell welcome to her! Still, as a gesture to the proprieties, his son Critchfield could accompany them, the son being good for little else (that he could see) except to be planted in the barn as a pissing-post.

Critch found the daily excursions happy ones. His mother always packed generous lunches – food that was far tastier than any she ever prepared at the hotel. She was also almost consistently good-humored, rarely giving way to the sudden flashes of temper which sent her blinding-quick hands out to slap and pinch and shake him. True, she was always sorry after these tantrums, as quick with pampering as she was with punishment. But while he forgave he could not completely forget, nor relax completely while she was within striking distance. He had never been able to, that is, until the advent of Ray Chance.

Critch was to marvel in later years that such a thorough-going scoundrel as Ray found it so easy to bring out all that was good and generous in people. But under analysis the trait seemed to be largely a matter of ignoring the grossest faults while praising the smallest virtues. Of turning negatives into affirmatives. Under Ray's magic, the ugliest dross became pure gold.

Ray never criticized his sniffling, but praised the manly manner in which he blew his nose. (*Almost had me blowing the damned thing off, Critch remembered wryly.*) Ray never remarked on his clumsiness, a tendency to trip over his own feet, but praised the fortitude which kept him tearless and unwhimper-ing. Ray had no jeers nor sneers for his thumb-sucking, his nervousness-inspired nail-biting. Merely remarking that it would be a shame to do anything which might mar the finest-looking hands he'd ever seen on a boy.

To demonstrate the strength and grace and other virtues which Ray and no other had ever observed in him, Critch took long runs across the prairie when they stopped during the noon hour. Leaping creeks and puddles. Jumping high in the Johnson grass and weeds tirelessly until he was only a speck in the distance. Winded, he came back much more slowly than he had gone, but that was all right, too. For Ray found much to admire in the way he conserved his strength when wisdom so dictated. Ray had many compliments for his ability to creep through the grass unseen (like a skilful hunter), then suddenly to spring up as if out of nowhere.

He was a lot better at creeping and sneaking than even Ray realized, several times approaching them so closely without their being aware of him that he saw things unintended for his eyes, and he knew he had better creep right back the way he had come from. But being a child and curious, his retreats were unhurried to say the least.

Ray and his mother were the first human beings he had seen at sexual intercourse. But he had witnessed it many times among the so-called lower animals, and none of life's innocent myths or intimate mysteries had survived the onslaught of Elizabethan nouns and verbs, which comprised much of Old Ike's vocabulary. So Critch well knew what he was seeing, even though the mechanics of it were new to him.

Ray was pounding his mother's meat. Ray was diddling his mother's pussy.

But why couldn't she accept it reasonably, as cattle and chickens did, instead of with such disgusting and annoying antics? Throwing her legs around Ray! Pitching and tossing with her butt until Ray was almost dislodged! Stretching and straining her big persimmon-tipped titties as she tried to force them to Ray's mouth! And laughing and crying at the same time, like nine kinds of a damn' fool! *Maybe she was part nigger, after all. Maybe?*

Old Ike had drifted through the Nations at a time when the Five Tribes were still slave-holders. And he had seen certain fleshly exhibitions which he still talked about with amusement and wonder. God damn! he would say. God damn, it was a pure marvel how one of them wenches could carry on when she got the bone in her!

A lady, now, she didn't like to do it. A lady just put up with it, because it was part of bein' a wife and mother, an' to keep it out of another hole. But them God damn nigger wenches! They could bust the balls on a dozen big bucks and still be hankerin' for more! It was the way they was built, y'know. All sap and rubber, and the more they used it the better it got (instead of gettin' loose as a goose like a lady's did).

Why, God damn, there was this one plenty-old wench. All of forty, if she was a day; practically toothless, with dugs as flat as a beetle's ass. But, by Christ, you just hold a cotton boll up to her crotch and see what happened! By Christ, she couldn't have plucked that boll any cleaner if she'd used her hands. Looked like a bush bunny had jumped up inside of her an' left his tail stickin' out.

A fact, by Christ! That's the way them wenches was. Built different, y'know. Not like ladies.

But like his mother? thought Critch.

That was the way niggers acted, wasn't it?

There came a day when Old Ike left King Junction before daylight for the long horseback ride to another village. Hardly was he out of sight before Critch, his mother and Ray also left – considerably earlier than they usually did – and with them went the contents of Ike King's strong box, stolen by his wife and secreted in the lunch hamper.

They traveled very fast, with none of the happy nonsense concomitant to their daily excursions. As the buggy sped over the rutted trail, the wheels rocking and dipping and jouncing, Critch was several times nearly thrown from his perch behind the lattice-backed seat. But his tentative protests and inquiries went unanswered by the two adults. And their unusual silence, the strained expressions on their faces, were more effective with Critch than any flattery or admonition could have been.

Something strange was going on. Something that was undoubtedly an extension of Ray's pounding of his mother's meat. Which was all right, by gosh, but if there was any fun in it they needn't think he was going to be left out of it!

It was early afternoon before they stopped. Not at one of the pleasant places they usually chose, but at a dismal line shack near the approximate eastern boundary of Old Ike's domain. Ray ate a sandwich while he fed and watered the horse. Critch pumped a drink for himself, warily accepted the parcel of food which his mother handed him and allowed her to lead him inside the shack.

There she stooped and put her arms around him. She hugged and kissed him many times, wept a little, and falteringly then firmly told him what he was to do.

Critch stared at her angrily. '*No!*' he shouted, so suddenly and loudly that she was almost rocked over backwards on her heels.

She started to strike him. 'Brat! Snotnose!' Then, bringing herself up with an effort, she became loving and pleading. But her son remained obdurate.

No, no, no! He *wasn't* going to stay there! Never mind the fact that she had left a note for his father, who would come and take him home. Never mind about his being a big brave boy. She wasn't foolin' him, by gosh!, and she was just a big old liar when

22

she said that she and Ray would be back in Junction City in no time at all and the three of them would have endless good times together.

'I'm goin' with you, because you ain't comin' back, never ever! You *can't* come back!'

'Now, Critch. Of course, we can, honey. Why do you—'

'Because! You an' Ray are married, so Papa can't be your husband no more!'

'Mar – Of course, we're not married!'

'You are so! You an' Ray been fuckin' so that makes you married!'

Ray appeared in the doorway at that moment, thus undoubtedly preventing Mrs. King from snatching her son baldheaded as she had often threatened to do. Ray said Critch was absolutely right; he and Critch's mother *were* married, and there was no reason in the world why Critch shouldn't go along with them and be their son.

'But, Ray—!' Mrs. King stared flabbergasted at her lover. 'We can't!'

'No? Think about it a moment. Think how much protection, a big, brave boy like Critch will be for us.' He winked at her. 'Well? Do you see it?'

'Well . . .'

'Ike is going to be pretty annoyed. If only we were involved, he just might arrange some unpleasantness. But as long as we have Critch with us . . .'

Critch went with them. Ray insisted on it. Nor did he apparently ever regret his decision, unless it was at the end of his career when he may have suspected Critch of his betrayal.

The boy was bright, malleable and anxious to please. One who was readily molded into the tasteful and personable pattern which he had arduously

23

created for himself. There was little if any immediate monetary reward for his careful tutelage of Critch. But Ray glimpsed a truly amazing potential in the youth, who would meanwhile fill his need for kindred companionship. He needed someone to talk to, someone who shared his likes and dislikes and his carefully acquired taste for the aesthetic. Ray's mother could satisfy none of those needs. The one she did fill was actually the least important to him.

Critch was pleasure and promise for Ray Chance. Critch enhanced his life. The woman, on the other hand, detracted from it, giving nothing but her tireless and increasingly tiresome loins.

Ray fancied himself as a master swindler, a man who achieved his ends by out-thinking his victims. He was not squeamish about the fatal employment of poisons and guns and knives, when they were necessary. But he felt a little demeaned in doing so, his great-thinker's image tarnished by the act of violence. And now, as a self-appointed model for the boy – a lad who literally worshipped him – he was unable to suffer the slightest smudge on his intrinsically tawdry escutcheon.

Alone, a swindler may 'work' single *or* double, temporarily acquiring a 'wife' or 'sister' if he chooses to do the latter. But a team, a man with a real or pseudo-encumbrance, must work double. Necessity – her mere presence – will force the woman into at least a minor role. She must be privy to her 'husband's' or 'brother's' affairs. Ignorance of them will spell disaster for them both.

So Ray launched one of the simplest confidence games. The supposed past-posting of a winning horse, on a race already run. He rehearsed his 'wife' in her tiny role until she appeared letter-perfect.

And, indeed, there was very little to rehearse. She had no more than a dozen words to say, before bursting into tears.

A few words, then the tears. What, for God's sake, could have been easier? A child could have done it, if the role had called for a child. Yet *she – she*, the stupid slut – blew it! She tipped the 'fool' she had roped, and the fool hollered copper.

Ray got them out of it, but not without an 'icing-off' of the law (the payment of bribes) which completely absorbed the remaining contents of Ike King's strongbox. Afterwards, she sulkily suggested that it wasn't her fault. He had made her nervous, and – brightly – she was sure she would do much better 'next time'. Ray was too furious to reply to this. But when they were alone that night, he beat her within an inch of her life.

He would have left her cold, except for his fear of losing Critch by doing so. He had to be surer of the boy than he was now; to weaken her hold on him while strengthening his own. And, dammit, she *must* be good for something besides screwing!

Bluntly speaking, however, she was good for little else. There was little else that she had been used for since her marriage to Ike at age thirteen. And, now, in her early thirties, such other talents as may have lain within her had become atrophied.

Ray was forced to accept her for what she was, and to make the best of it. It did not work out too badly for a time.

She was sweet bait for the badger game. An over-the-shoulder look at a fool, then a sensuous twist of her hips, and she had him in her bedroom. Into which, of course, her outraged 'husband' would burst at a crucial moment.

Money-wise, they began to 'get well,' as the saying was. But, gradually, repetition brought boredom to her, making her into a preposterous facsimile of the errant and frightened wife she was supposed to be. Instead of cowering, she was apt to yawn. Once she had even squatted on the pot, mumbling her pleas for forgiveness to the tinkle of urine.

Ray lectured her, pointing out their terrible physical danger, the certain fiscal disaster, which must derive from her attitude. He beat her, frustration adding to his fury as he sensed her gratification at the punishment. But neither scoldings nor beatings could change her. Just as boredom, too much of a sameness, had driven her from old Ike, it was now taking her off on another tangent. And at the worst possible time. They needed to hit big, or at least steady, yet in the sorry sum of her moments, there was no jackpot.

Descent is easy. One must rest before the long climb upward, and the best place is always on the next step down. There is no hurry, no cause for alarm. After all, what goes down must come up, mustn't it?

Well?

She made a good whore, the runaway wife of Old Ike King. Her reputation for giving satisfaction spread so rapidly that Ray had to do no pimping once he had started her. For here, in sameness, she found variety. In sameness, she found a challenge. Something which lent itself to delightful testing and experimentation, with unfailing reward to her senses.

She made a good whore . . . as a practitioner. One who was more and more pleased and pleasing with each transaction. And that was the trouble with her. Here, as in everything else, she defeated herself.

It was enough for her, the act itself. She meant to demand money; usually she did demand it. But often, in the excitement and anticipation of the moment, she forgot to. And when she did not, well, a little toying with her by a patron, a pretense of being broke or disinterested, would make her drop her demands. Some men even boasted that they had got her to *pay them*. The only complaint ever made against her was that she plumb wore a fella out.

At fourteen, Critch had known for some time that his mother was getting it pounded for money, and he unemotionally accepted the fact as a necessary fact of life. She did it with Ray? Why not with others? He was dependent on her for support; without her earnings his ever-fascinating association with Ray would be impossible. And, so he was grateful to her. Perhaps, in the deepest recesses of his mind, there was buried a sickish shame. Perhaps, also, there was anger and hatred for Ray for bringing her to this. But these feelings were well-buried. Things so deeply sunk in the subconscious that they must twist tortuously to the surface, distorted (and distorting) and manifesting themselves in attitudes unidentifiable with their source.

He was still fourteen when his mother was lost to him. Lost twice. The second time was when she fled him and Ray with a pimp, never to be seen or heard of again. The first time . . .

Well, that was the only time that counted. For she had ceased to exist for him after that. After that, he blotted her out of his mind, for he could not think of her without vomiting.

He had gone to sleep late on the night in question. Ray and his mother were arguing violently in the adjoining room, making sleep impossible. Finally,

27

their voices died and he dozed off, but not for long. He came awake with a sudden start, a sick chill creeping up his spine at the strange sounds from the other room.

He had never heard anything like them before. Which was natural enough. It was only during the last year or so, during the restless dawning of puberty, that he could stay awake after ten at night. Only during the last year or so, whereas his mother had been whoring for more than two years. And a whore may not be bruised and battered without lessening her income. Ray had managed to restrain himself. Tonight, however, Ray had been pushed too far. He had nothing to lose by beating her, that he could see. The silly bitch had been busy all day. One customer after another. Yet she'd wound up the day with less than she'd had at the outset. Her money given away along with her body. Free ass and money to go with it!

She lay sprawled on the bed on her stomach, scanty gown drawn up over the flaring buttocks which Ray, teeth gritted in his white face, was promising to beat off of her.

He raised his belt high; brought it down with a slashing *craack!* upon the rounded hummocks of naked flesh. They quivered and squirmed, delicate shivers running through them like things with an existence of their own and distinct from the rest of her body. Ray paused, panting for breath. There was silence, motionlessness for a moment, while the dimmed coal-oil lamp flickeringly limned the scene: a lewd nightmare by a drunken Doré. Then, there was a slight twitching of the undulant sand-colored torso; a small impatient movement. And from the

28

pillows came a muffled sob: querulous, questioning. Prompting.

Ray's eyes blazed. The belt whipped up and down, up and down, furiously raining blows upon the ever-hungering flesh. And, silently, the door to the adjoining room opened, and Critch looked in on them.

He moved instinctively, without a split-second's thought. A simple reaction to Ray's action. Hurling himself between this man and his mother; automatically stopping what had to be stopped, as the blink of an eyelid stops a probing. Because it must. Because there is great loss if it is not.

And then, looking up at Ray, a little frightened by what he had done. Frightened and apologetic. Yet still driven by an inbred urge, he struck feebly at his idol, causing the man to fall back a step.

'Y-You can't do that,' he quavered. 'You don't . . . y-you can't – mustn't hit a woman.'

The voice was his, but the words, the long-age injunction, at least, were his father's. A she, girl or woman, could not be hit. It might make her titties rot or screw-up her innards (which were plenty screwed-up to begin with, and not like the good guts of a man). *I ever catch you hittin' another gal, boy, I'll yank off your pecker an' flog you t' death with it*. The Apache, Tehapa, Old Ike's oldest and dearest friend, had endorsed the tabu against the hitting of shes, although he had privately added a qualification. It was bad medicine to beat woman (just as it was bad to beat young children, when their peters and pussies were still inside them and might be injured thereby). But there *were* occasions when it was not only well but necessary to *kill* a woman. This was so, and all wise men knew it.

29

And now, Critch looked up at Ray fearfully and apologetically. But stubbornly, with a sense of righteousness. 'You can't, Ray,' he stammered. 'I'm s-sorry, but you mustn't.'

'No?' Ray smiled, cocking a quizzical brow. 'Now, why is that, hmmm?'

'Because!'

'Yes? Why because?'

'You know. Because it's – it's—'

Critch couldn't find the words to explain. Given time, he might have conjured them from the shadows of the past, but he was not given time.

His mother was suddenly behind him, knotting furious fingers in his hair. Giving him a twirling yank that sent him staggering across the room to come up solidly against the wall.

He slid down the wall, sat down on the floor with a small thud. A little dizzily he stared at the hate-filled face of his mother. And words came to him from the mouth of that face, a torrent of filth from the whore's vocabulary.

Mothersuckin' turd, grannygobbler, jismeater, screwing little shit. 'What d'ya mean, huh? Hah? What d'ya mean hittin' Ray? I'll learn you, yuh bastard! Beat the fuckin' piss out of yuh!'

She started toward him, hesitated; sidled an approval-seeking glance at Ray. His face was expressionless, and she humbly lifted his hand and tried to kiss it.

He pulled it away from her. Crossing the room to Critch, he held the hand down to him. Hesitantly, Critch took it and was helped to his feet, his eyes shifting between his mother and Ray. Between woman and man. Scowling whore and smiling gentleman.

'You see how it is, Critch? You try to help her, and you see what happens? You see? You see what happens?'

Critch stared at the woman. She stared back at him stolidly, scornfully. And then her expression changed, and then it changed again. And again and again and again, as its owner sought to adjust and sort out, and find some verity that could be lived with. And at last finding only what there was to be found, all that there ever is for anyone, be it gold or base-metal or merely dross. But inevitably acceptable, in any case, because that is all there is and there is no more.

She accepted it as she had at the beginning. A worst that was still the best. Eyes narrowed sensuously, painted mouth parted with promise, she lay back down on the bed and rolled over on her stomach.

'Critch?' Ray held out the belt, smiling. 'It's all right, Critch.'

Critch looked at the belt. He looked at the woman on the bed, and back again. Numbly; frozen. His emotions locked on dead-center in this endless moment in time. They caught there, caught between the irresistible force of heredity and the immovable object of circumstance. How can one move, when there is no place to move to?

As if from a great distance, a sound came to his ears. A faint creak, a fainter slithering. Terrified, fighting with everything that was in him, Critch struggled to hold his gaze steady, to keep it from moving to the bed. Yet little by little, that something that was at the very core of his being crumbled and gave way, and silently screaming he went over the precipice.

The sleazily revealing nightgown was slowly sliding upward. Slowly, so slowly, like the faulty curtain on a play.

First, there was only the hint of a shadowy cleft. Then, with a small jerk, a definite glimpse of it; the beginning of a cleavage which widened gradually as the gown slid higher and higher. Now, twin hillocks of softness; sand-colored, swelling and flaring, and curving in to the tiny waist. Now, the shadowy canyon shallowing between those hillocks; tapering, as they curved, into the faintest of indentations, and disappearing entirely at the dimpled base of her spine . . .

No more then.

Never any more for Critch. After this, there would never be anything. Nothing that would make him draw back, or prod tellingly at his conscience.

'You see how it is, Critch? You see?'

I see.

'Beat that yellow ass, boy! Pound that pretty tail!'

Critch took the belt.

b

Mr. Isaac Joshua King,
King Junction,
Oklahoma Territory.

Dear Sir:
This is to urge you to ignore the highly complimentary letter anent your son, Critchfield, which I wrote you earlier today, as I have since found that my endorsement of him was wholly unwarranted. These are the circumstances:
While having refreshments with your son, I suddenly

discovered that my wallet was missing. With apparent generosity he paid our bill with a ten-dollar banknote, and I thought no more of the incident until several hours later – after I had written my first letter to you – when I was called upon by the proprietor of the establishment we had visited. He had the ten-dollar banknote, a worthless wildcat, with him. Since it had been spent by a companion of mine, though a stranger to him, he wished me to make good on it (which, of course, I did).

Now, sir, I remember this particular banknote well. I had carried it in my wallet for a long time, more or less as a souvenir, and I had marked it in a distinctive fashion as a reminder that I was not to spend it. There could not possibly be two such bills with two such markings. Under the circumstances, there cannot be the slightest doubt that your son, Critchfield, stole my wallet.

I don't know how or when he did it. Nor do I know why such a prepossessing young man, who is obviously not in the slightest need of money, would stoop to thievery. Yet the damning truth is clear, and there can be no denying it.

> With sincere regrets,
> Washington Dying Horse
> Attorney-at-law

c

It was almost noon, of the fourth day after the theft, and Critch was still in Tulsa. A deadly inertia had gripped him, one born of funk and the fear of failure, and he could not move himself to do what he must do.

He paced the floor of his cheap hotel room, the cheapest which the smallest claim to fastidiousness had allowed him to take. Desperately, he slammed the fist of one hand into the palm of the other.

Taking out his billfold, he again recounted its contents.

Not enough, he thought ruefully, returning the wallet to his pocket. Rather, there was barely enough for the basics of his plan. By the time he paid his modest hotel bill and bought his ticket to King's Junction, he would be just about broke. Maybe a few dollars left over for food and a few drinks along the way, but no more than that. He'd be broke when he reached the junction. Which simply meant that the trip would be wasted. For he'd won only half the battle in his acceptance by Attorney Dying Horse.

Old Ike King was the one who had to be convinced. Old Ike, with his thousands upon thousands of valuable acres and the untold wealth that went with them.

Ike King would accept no one as his heir who was not completely worthy – worthy by *his* standards. And those standards would be extremely rigid where Critch was concerned. He was under a very big cloud, was Critch. The old man would have him identified with his wife's faithlessness and treachery. Only success, money – concrete proof that he had risen far above this evil disadvantage – would satisfy Ike.

Or maybe not, Critch thought hopefully. Maybe I'm being too hard on him. After all, I haven't seen him in thirteen years. So maybe . . .

Maybe nothing. The fact that he'd been away for thirteen years was the trouble. Old Ike hadn't been able to keep tabs on him, as he had with his sons Arlington and Bosworth. Arlie, who was a year older than Critch, and Boz, who was a year older than Arlie, had remained with their father all these years. Working on his vast holdings, unquestioningly doing his bidding. And they'd damned well managed to please him – to prove their right to be his heirs – or Old Ike would have kicked them out. He, Critch, on the other hand . . .

Critch grinned wryly, his mind sliding off on a tangent as he thought of the high-sounding names.

Critchfield, Arlington and Bosworth. His mother had copied them from the hotel register. As stupid as she was, it was a damned good thing that there'd been no travelers named Screwingwell or Fartsinajug!

His moth – he jerked his thoughts away from her. Brought them back to his two brothers.

Arlie and Boz. They'd have to be killed, of course. All of something was infinitely better than a third. And he could never be sure of even a third as long as his brothers lived. The old man might draw unflattering comparisons between them and him. He just might decide to disinherit the youngest son. On the other hand, if only that youngest son were alive, with no one else to inherit . . .

Yes, Arlie and Boz would have to go. He would have to kill them. And murdering Boz, at least, would be a positive pleasure. A mean bastard, that Boz. Senselessly mean. Always twisting your arms or bending back your fingers or jabbing you with a stick. Any damned thing to hear you holler. Old Iké had caught him skinning a live kitten one day, and he'd had the kitten cooked for Boz's supper. And he'd made him eat it, too. Old Ike would give him a crack with a horsewhip every time he'd stopped eating; never letting up on his son until he'd begun vomiting blood. But that still didn't let Boz off the hook. He was allowed to stop eating, but only for that night. He got cat for breakfast the next morning and every meal after that – no other food, by God – until he'd eaten every damned bit of it.

And even that didn't change Boz a bit. He'd gotten sneakier, harder to catch in his nastiness, but he was meaner than ever.

Critch had acquired the learning and maturity of mind to understand why Boz was as he was. He'd never forgiven his brother, but he did understand him. As the oldest son, he'd caught the full force of his father's sternness, excruciatingly dulling it with his hide and making it bearable for his younger brothers. As the oldest, more had been demanded of him. When he couldn't deliver, promptly and perfectly, Old Ike had landed on him. So, inevitably, Boz had turned mean. Helpless against his father's wrath, Boz had turned his own rage against other helpless things.

As for Arlington – Arlie – well, his demise would genuinely trouble Critch (though not enough to keep him from bringing it off). Most middle-children get relatively little attention, as compared with a family's youngest and oldest, suffering neither spoiling nor strictness. Thus, they develop as a benign nature dictates they should – giving happiness to get it, being pleasing to be pleased – and they usually turn out well.

Arlie was hard and tough, as any son of Old Ike would have to be. But along with it he was good-natured and helpful. A nice guy. Or so Critch thought of him . . .

Now, Critch jumped up from the bed with a curse. Angrily telling himself that it was time to get moving.

He had to do something – *something*, by God! – and he had to do it now. Lifting his two expensive bags to the bed, he impatiently sorted through them, inven-

36

torying the expensive suits and shirts, and all the other accoutrements of a well-heeled gentleman.

He finished his assay; stood frowning, his eyes narrowed in thought. A lot of valuable stuff, but it wouldn't bring much at a second-hand store. Wouldn't do to sell it, anyway, since, as much as money, he needed the appearance. Once a man lost his front, he couldn't operate.

There *was* one thing, now. The watch. The impressively embossed watch, with its studding of sparkling stones, which bore a famous and honored name.

Critch lifted it from his Gladstone and held it up for examination. A watch like that was worth five hundred dollars – as any fool could see. Rather, it would have been worth five hundred, *if* it had been the gold that it appeared to be, and *if* the apparent diamonds had been real, and *if* the brand name had been genuine instead of counterfeit.

The trouble with selling a thing like this was that (1) you had to claim ownership, and (2) a professional estimate of its value was invariably called for. Oh, of course, you could probably unload it on someone for a quick double sawbuck. But expert fakery like this was costly, and turning it for a twenty would be little more than a matter of swapping dollars.

The watch couldn't be sold, then. It was his one bet, but he could attempt no scheme with it which might bring trouble. Too much was at stake, and he was simply too funky to face trouble.

What he needed was a fool, a prize Grade-A chump. One who could be cashed in fast and heavily. And in a way which could not possibly bring a kickback.

Where was one most likely to find such a fool?

What was the way whereby said fool could be safely cashed in?

Critch's scowl of concentration suddenly disappeared, and a slow smile spread over his handsome face.

d

She had come in on the train from the north some thirty minutes ago. A young woman, judging by what he could glimpse through her filmly half veil. He couldn't see much of her face; and her clothes, odds and ends of ill-fitting stuff, pretty well concealed her body. But whether she was attractive or well-shaped didn't matter. In all the things that did matter, she seemed to fit the bill.

A fool traveling alone. A fool with a couple of pretty nice bags. Getting off the train from the north, she'd come into the station with timidity-slumped shoulders, and glanced around with quick shyness. Then she'd retired to a bench well away from everyone else, and she'd been sitting there ever since. Head-ducked, hands clenched in her lap. So frightened and nervous by these strange surroundings that she'd probably jump if you said boo to her.

She hadn't traveled far: wasn't sufficiently rumpled and smoke-smeared to have come from any great distance. But her manner and the two heavy bags indicated that she had some distance to go. Critch felt the train-ticket nestled in an inner pocket of his tailored coat, wondering if he could possibly be as lucky as the signs seemed to indicate.

- He'd bought the ticket, intending to cash it in if he had to, to the army-base town of Lawton. Buying it at an excursion rate and getting it much cheaper than the fare to King's Junction, which was a shorter distance away. Now, if this scared-to-death little skirt was also going to Lawton—

Well, it didn't matter too much either way. She was obviously a fool who could be cashed in for something.

Critch straightened his shoulders. He came briskly out of the shadowed recess from which he had been studying her, looked sharply around the waiting room in the manner of a man seeking someone, then allowed himself to see her. She seemed to make herself smaller under his stare. Frowning, keeping his eyes fixed on her shrinking figure, Critch strode across the waiting room and sat down next to her.

'May I see your ticket?' he said firmly.

'W-wha—' A frightened gasp from behind the veil. 'W-why – what—?'

'Your ticket please! Let me see it.'

He held out his hand. She fumbled open her purse, allowing him a quick look at the comfortable roll of bills inside, and almost snatched out the ticket.

Critch took it, and examined it at length. His pulse quickening a little as he saw its destination.

Lawton – Fort Sill. A soldier's wife or prospective bride, or kin. And she'd never been there before, obviously, or she wouldn't be so nervous about it.

'Going to Fort Sill, eh?' He handed back the ticket. 'Is that your home?'

'N-no, sir. It's Kan – I mean, Missouri.'

'Yes?' – very sharply.

'M-Missouri. Kansas City, Missouri.'

She gave him the street address; then, with a frightened little rush, told him her name. Anderson, Anne Anderson. And she was the wife of Private

39

John Anderson, and they'd been married when he was home on furlough, and now she was going to join him, and – and—

'Now, now, dear . . .' Smiling warmly, he cut her off. 'I'm Captain Crittenden, base legal officer at the post. Perhaps you've heard your husband speak of me? Well, at any rate, I had to establish who you were and be sure you were an honest person, because . . .'

Because of this valuable watch he'd found at the entrance to the depot. (A beauty, wasn't it? Solid gold, with diamonds.) The station agent didn't look very reliable to him. Probably say he was going to turn the watch over to the rightful owner, and never do it – and how could he, the Captain, be sure it was done after he'd gone on his way? He'd made a few inquiries on his own without any luck, and now he had business up in town for a few minutes. So as long as she was going to be here, anyway, would she mind keeping the watch in case the owner showed up?

'Oh, no! I mean, oh, yes, of course, I'll do it!' She was almost tearful with relief at the abrupt warming of his attitude. 'I'll stay right here! That's a promise, Captain, and you can depend on it! I – I mean, you don't need to worry—'

'Of course, I don't, dear.' He gave her hand a paternal squeeze. 'I'm a lawyer, remember? I know a fine young woman when I see her.' He started to rise; hesitated. 'By the way, I'm afraid I was pretty brusque when I first spoke to you. I – well, my wife passed away a couple of weeks ago, and . . .'

'Oh, how terrible! I'm so sorry, Captain.'

'Thank you,' he said, with simple sincerity, adding that he was even now returning from his wife's funeral in the east. 'As I was about to say, however,

I've noticed that I sometimes do become a little curt with people since her death, and if I did, in your case—'

But he hadn't been! Not in the least teensiest bit, Captain!

'Thank you, my dear,' he said. 'You're a dear, sweet girl.'

He left her, with a tip of his fine Fedora hat. Some twenty minutes later, after a time-killing stroll, he returned to the station.

True to her promise, she had remained exactly where he had left her. He resumed his seat at her side, smilingly pointing out that she had proved his merits as a judge of honest people. She squirmed pleasurably at the compliment, ducking her head with a little giggle. She started to return the watch, but he affably declined it. After all, there was more room in her purse than there was in his pockets, and women were much better at taking care of things than men were.

'Just don't see how you do it,' he declared in assumed amazement. 'Why, my wife can—' He broke off; turned his head for a moment as though to dispel a tear. Then, softly, 'Isn't it strange? She was so much a part of me that I just can't believe she's gone.'

'Why, you poor thing!' she said; then abashed at her daring, 'Oh, excuse me, Captain! I – I—'

'Now, now, dear Anne. There's no rank between friends. Sorrow makes equals of us all.'

'Sorrow makes – I think that's the most beautiful thing I ever heard, Captain! So, uh, poetic kind of. D-Do you like poetry, Captain?'

Critch confessed that it was a weakness of his, and that he sometimes wrote it. 'Perhaps you've heard one of my little efforts, *Roses Are Red And Violets Are Blue*.'

'Oh, my goodness, yes! My goodness! Have you written any others, Captain?'

Critch nodded indulgently, and gave her a couple of verses of burlesque-house pathos. She was so impressed, so awed, that only with an effort did he suppress the lurking imp within him and its insistent demand that he tell her about the old hermit named Dave, who had kept a dead whore in his cave.

'Well, now . . .' He stretched his legs, glancing at the octagon-faced station clock. 'A long wait until train time, isn't it? Well, over an hour yet. I think you and I shall just get us a good bite of dinner.'

She demurred. She really wasn't a bit hungry, and, uh, really she'd just rather stay where she was. Oh, no. It wasn't because of the money, but—

'Of course, it isn't. You'll be my guest, naturally. Now, you just go over there' – nodding toward the ladies room – 'and give yourself a good freshing up. You'll want to do that, I assume' – a kindly but critical look. 'Travel does so smear up a person.'

She arose reluctantly, started to reach for her two heavy bags. Critch grandly waved her away from them.

'I'll just check them through to your destination while you're gone. Did you know you could do that? Much safer than they would be with you, and you're saved a lot of trouble.'

'Well, uh, but—'

'Yes? Like to get something out of them first?'

'No, but—'

But nothing. She had the watch, didn't she? That solid, gold, diamond-studded watch.

42

'F-Fine, Captain. Thanks very much. I'll hurry right back.'

'Oh, take your time, dear,' Critch smilingly urged her. 'Take your time. We'll be dining in a very nice place, and I want you to look your prettiest.'

She bobbed her head, moved away from him with her shyly stooped shoulders and timidly lowered face. Critch waited until she disappeared through the swinging doors of the restroom. Then, he carried her baggage out a side entrance, and down the street a few doors to a combination pawnshop-secondhand store.

Critch had learned of the place from other professionals on the criminal circuit. Between the *right* people, there was a ready exchange of such information. He had had no occasion to do business with the establishment's proprietor heretofore, but he had stopped by for a chat. And today the latter gestured Critch toward the back room, then joined him behind its curtained portals after a quick look up and down the street.

'No one following you, huh? Well, let's take a look at it.'

The contents of the two bags were of a type with the oddly-assorted stuff which the girl had been wearing. The kind of things which only ignorant unworldliness would allow. Or perhaps they had been wished on her by well-meaning relatives. They weren't intrinsically shoddy; someone, if not her, had laid out some bucks for them. They just weren't suitable; a lot of everything, but not one good everyday outfit. Why, hell, there were even a couple of party gowns! Did she think Fort Sill was West Point?

'Well . . .' The proprietor measured a gown against his own squatty body; shook his head dubiously. 'I dunno about the rags, but the luggage ain't bad. Call it thirty?'

'Call it forty.'

'Call me Santy Claus,' said the proprietor, and he counted out the forty.

And, meanwhile, in a stall of the women's restroom, Emma Allerton, alias Anne Anderson, stood naked from the waist up. Her shoulders thrown back, her abundant bosom rising and falling with the unaccustomed pleasure of deep breathing.

Christ, what a relief! What a relief to get out of that harness for a while and straighten up!

She stretched luxuriously, sucking her stomach in and out, pulling her chin in for a critical glance at her nakedness. *Bet I know what you'd like to have, she told it. And her groin prickled at the thought.* Then, her gaze fell on her right breast, at the rough furrow of teeth marks where once had been the nipple. And she cursed in silent fury.

The horny old bastard! Every time she saw that bub she got mad all over. Goddamn him! Goddam her sister!

It was really Sis's fault, the overbearing slut! Sis should have given the guy the hatchet long before. But she'd been having too much fun in the next room, so Emma-Annie had got her tit chomped.

A hell of a sister, Sis was. But she'd paid for it, by Jesus. Oh, but she'd paid for it! Rather, Little Sis had paid herself, and just in time, too, from what she'd heard. The news hadn't hit the papers yet, but the grapevine had it that the law had either grabbed Sis or was just about to do it.

Anne patted the thick money belt which cinched

her waist, eyes bright with malice as she thought of her sister. Absently, she allowed a hand to stray over the mutilated breast, and in her mind it became another's hand, and her expression softened dreamily.

Damn, it would be nice after all these weeks. Six weeks of running, crossing and crisscrossing the Mid-West and Southwest, leaving a trail that was no trail, and then finally swinging down into the Territory. Six weeks of going around with her head ducked and her chest caved in, and looking like something the cat dug up.

No sport in all that time. And none that was really worth having before then. Sis had always taken on the good-looking guys, and forced the clodhoppers on her. Not once had she ever gotten a crack at a guy even half as cute and handsome as Captain Crittenden.

He remained in her mind as she reluctantly regarbed herself. Thinking what a damned shame it was that things were as bad as they were.

If she hadn't claimed to be married, practically a new bride—

If he hadn't just lost his wife—

With a regretful little shake of her head, she finished dressing. She started to leave the stall, then sat down on the stool and crossed one leg over the other. Her shoes were high-topped and laced, in the style of the day. With a sharp twist of her hand, she removed the heel of one of them.

It was hollow, and a tiny Derringer nestled within it. Reassured, she replaced the heel, smoothed out her skirt and left the stall. And once again her mind moved from business to pleasure.

Captain Crittenden.

Was it really as unthinkable as it seemed?

He was kind of dumb, in a cute way, and he would be vain like all men. So why shouldn't he suddenly find himself in the saddle, and why shouldn't she suddenly find herself playing horsie, without either of them – heaven forbid! – ever, ever meaning for it to happen?

Smiling, he came swiftly toward her as she emerged from the restroom. Guiding her out of the station, he complimented her on her appearance, giving her various little pats and squeezes – amiably innocent actions which unerringly detected the money belt. With the same ostensible inadvertence, she nudged him with a breast and rubbed a buttock against his thigh.

Arm in arm, Anne-Emma, professional murderess, and Critch-Captain Crittenden, arch scoundrel, moved companionably toward their date with destiny.

CHAPTER THREE

a

In their bedroom at the King's Junction Hotel (which was also the King ranch-house) Old Ike's oldest son, Boz, grabbed the firm round breast of his Apache wife, Joshie – old Tepaha's grand-daughter – and twisted it cruelly. Twisting it harder and harder, gritting threats to rip it off of her. And the girl still remained coldly stoical. Silent, motionless; refusing to recognize the torture of her husband's presence by even the smallest moan or movement.

At last, he desisted, shifting from brutality to a kind of argumentative pleading. Making a feeble attempt at caressing her in the pre-dawn darkness.

'Aah, c'm on now, Joshie. Why'nt you admit it, huh? You warned him, didn't you? You told ol' Arlie that I was trying to get him.'

'Hah!' the girl spat out the word. 'I your squaw. You think I tell on sonabitch husband?'

'Well, how did he find out then, huh? How'd he figger it out if you didn't tell him?'

'How he figger out skunk make bad stink?'

'Why, you God damn—!'

'Arlie smarter'n you, old Boz. Old Arlie plenty man.'

'Shit! You sayin' I ain't a man?'

'I say it. You got no balls.'

Boz cursed, started to reach out for her again.

47

Then knowing the uselessness of it, he angrily flopped over on his back.

And in their bedroom at the King's Junction Hotel (which was also the King ranch-house) Arlie grasped his wife, Kay – for King – who was also Tepaha's grand-daughter and Joshie's sister, and gave her naked bottom an admiring slap.

'Now, that's an ass,' he declared. 'Get's any bigger you'll be shittin' in a washtub.'

'Ho!' Kay giggled happily. 'I shit in your hand, old husband.'

'Now, God damn if you ain't a snotty ol' squaw!'

'You like snotty ol' squaw?' She snuggled close to him, sneaking a small hand across his hard, flat belly. 'You like ol' squaw's stuff?'

'Well, now, I ain't so sure that I do. Maybe I just better take me a little sample . . .'

After they had again separated their bodies, and lay contentedly side by side, Kay whispered in her husband's ear; nudging him with playful impatience when he did not immediately answer.

'You do it, huh, ol' Arlie? You kill sonabitch Boz today?'

'We-el' – Arlie paused, teasing her. 'Well, I reckon so. Figger I'll have me a plenty good chance today.'

'How you do it?'

Arlie shrugged lazily, murmuring that he'd kind of have to wait and see. 'But if I know that son-of-a-bitch, he's practically gonna do it for me.'

'Just you do it,' Kay insisted; then, wife-like. 'You too good-natured. Let people put things over on you.'

Arlie said he was going to put something over on her in about a moment. Kay persisted in her nagging.

'You get Critch, too. He come, you kill him.'

'Critch? What the hell for?'

'Hah! Same reason kill sonabitch, Boz.'

'Now, God damn,' drawled Arlie, in admiring wonderment. 'Ain't you the bloodthirsty ol' squaw! Don't even know whether Critch is comin', an' already you're after me to kill him.'

'Must make plans,' Kay said smugly. 'Must be ready.'

'Keep it up,' Arlie warned her. 'You just keep on talkin', an' I'll show you some plans. Danged good ones, too.'

'Ho! You not ready, old husband. Too soon.'

Arlie faced around to her, gave her bottom another smack. 'Real sure of that, are you? Real, real sure?'

'Well . . . Maybe you show me?'

b

Behind the closed double-doors of the hotel ranchhouse bar room, Tepaha, the Apache, and Isaac Joshua King, blustered and snarled at one another. Old Ike called Tepaha a woman with a peter. Old Tepaha declared that Ike had done treachery to a friend and brother.

'Even a boast you have made of it!' the old Indian shouted. 'You were warmed at Geronimo's fire. You smoked with him, and he called you friend and brother, and you smiled and called him like-wise. And then' – Tepaha raised his arm dramatically. 'Then you—'

'Silence!' Old Ike cut him off with an infuriated howl. 'You twist truth into lies! I told you how it was! A hundred times, I told you! Why the hell don't you get the straight of it?'

'Shit!' said Tepaha loudly. 'Old Ike is old shit!'

It was a favorite word of his; one that he found extremely useful (as did Ike). Depending on how, where and when it was used, it could be virtually a vocabulary by itself.

'Goin' to tell you one more time,' Old Ike said. 'Ain't gonna tell it again, so by God you better listen . . .'

'Shit!'

'Will you hear me, old fool! The bluecoats had Geronimo in a cage there at Fort Sill. In a cage, by God, like a *chongo* in a zoo. An' all the God damn' saddle-tramps an' nesters an' their God damn' families for miles around had come in to gawk an' poke fun at him. Well, by Christ, I didn't like it a damn bit, an' I let 'em know it. I pushed my way through 'em, knockin' a few of 'em down, by God, an' I called Geronimo my friend and brother, like he was, o' course, an' I put my hand through the bars to shake with him. An' you know what that dirty *chongo* Apache done?'

'*Chongo*,' taunted Old Tepaha. 'Apache monkey, you monkey, too. You Apache brother.'

'That God damn' – *shut up!* – that God damn' Geronimo grabbed my hand and bit it! So, by Christ, I just got me a-hold of the bastard's nose, an' I damn' near twisted if off'n him before the bluecoats butted in. An' – an' I ain't a damn' bit sorry, neither!'

But he was sorry. He had acted instinctively, without stopping to think that Geronimo's eyes and ears were probably failing him, and he had judged Old Ike yet another enemy instead of his friend and brother.

He was sorry as hell, Old Ike was. And Tepaha was sorry that he had raised the subject. He had done so out of friendship and pride – the same motives

50

which had moved Old Ike to taunt and abuse him. For great shame had come to the families of Tepaha and King; a particularly degrading shame, since a member of each family had offended against a member of the other family. Boz was known to have abused his wife, Joshie. I.K. – Tepaha's grandson – had been caught stealing from his 'Uncle,' Old Ike.

It is unforgivable to steal from family. From others, it is all right, even commendable. Though Old Ike's thinking, as regards the latter, was not quite so liberal as it once had been.

At any rate, they had been shamed – and even now they waited to mete out stern punishment to the guilty ones – and out of their deep hurt they acted as they did. To divert one another. To boldly prove that they were above hurt. For it is insulting to offer pity to a man, and disgraceful to appear to be in need of it.

Tepaha stirred the fire in the potbellied stove. Old Ike poured drinks for them and lit a cigar, and held the match for his friend.

Though their brotherhood was by choice, rather than the accident of birth, a stranger might have thought otherwise despite their differences in coloring. For they had been together for so many years and in so many places, sharing the same thoughts and deeds, that, in their necessary adjustment to one another, each had borrowed of the other's mannerisms and expressions, and now they had come to look quite a little alike.

Much of the time, even their talk was strikingly similar, Ike's alleged English even becoming a trifle broken. He was almost as fluent in Apache as Tepaha; also in idiomatic Spanish. And they spoke in both languages frequently – often sounding so much alike that it was hard to tell when one finished and the other began.

Old Ike shaved his head regularly, while Tepaha's hair grew to the lobes of his ears; and he wore a beaded band around his forehead whereas Old Ike wore a sombrero. But both men were clothed in calf-hide jackets, and levis. And both were shod in blockheeled Spanish boots; and protruding from the right boot of each was the worn haft of a gleaming knife.

As Old Ike sighed, unconsciously, Tepaha demanded another reading of the letters from crazy Osage lawyer. Brightening, Old Ike hauled the letters from his pocket, and both chuckled over them as they were read yet another time.

'Damn' crazy Osage,' Ike concluded. 'Says right here that Critch is plenty fine fella, got plenty o' money. Then he tries to claim Critch stole a stinkin' fifty dollars from him! What kind of God damn' sense does that make?'

'All Osage crazy,' Tepaha nodded wisely. 'Critch do right to steal money.'

'Well, I don't know as I'd say that, but . . .'

He shook his head, lapsed back into silence, his mouth sagging. Tepaha requested another reading of the letters. Old Ike ignored him. Nor could he be baited into another quarrel.

And, then, at last, when Tepaha was at his wits' end to help his friend, inspiration came to him. From far back in the all-but-forgotten past it came, and it proved highly effective in rousing Old Ike from his reverie.

'Huh! What the hell did you say?' He glared beetle-browed at Tepaha. 'What d'ya mean, I et him?'

'I mean,' said Tepaha, with simulated spitefulness. 'I mean what I say. You eat Osage.'

'That's a God damn' lie! I never et no one, Indian or white! I don't hold with eatin' people!'

'Eat 'em, anyway. You eat – Wait!' He held up a hand, chopping off the incipient outburst from his friend. 'Take yourself back many, many years. So many years, until that good time when we were young. Remember it, Old Ike – the night we saw Geronimo for the first time? The night we were brought into his lodge at lance-point? We had come up from *Tejas* to *okla homa*, the Land of the Red Man . . .'

c

They had crossed Red River, the boundary between Oklahoma and Texas, that morning; losing their pack-horses and supplies to the river's quicksands, almost losing their lives as they fruitlessly tried to free the screaming animals. By luck and by God, as the saying was, they had somehow managed to get their mounts into deep water and swim them to the north shore. But their powder was a muddy mess, useless for their long Sharps rifles. And it was snowing; and the frozen short-grassed prairie was barren of game.

Tepaha dug into the dry center of an ancient buffalo turd, and got it lighted with his steel and flint. They fed the flame with more dung, and dried their clothes enough to keep them from freezing. Then, they headed north again, unarmed save for their knives, their heads ducked against the blowing snow.

By night the storm had become a blizzard. But

there was the faint smell of smoke ahead of them, the scent of cooking food; and rocking in their high-pommeled saddles, they urged their trembling horses onward. An hour passed. The smell of food and smoke was still ahead of them. And around them, all-but-inaudible in the howling wind, were sounds. Sounds that were felt rather than heard. Shallow breaks in silence which Ike and Tepaha had trained themselves to become aware of and to interpret for what they were, as requisite to life.

Silently, they drew their knives. At virtually the same instant their horses reared upward, startled as their bridles were suddenly grabbed by unseen hands. Then – Well, nothing, then. Nothing more than a couple of butted lances, which connected solidly with the skulls of Tepaha and Ike King and knocked them senseless from their saddles.

They were prodded and kicked to their feet.

The lance-points pricking incessantly at their rumps, they were run into the village of the Apache leader, Geronimo, and on to the great lodge of Geronimo himself.

The Indian chief at that time was probably in his middle forties, or approximately twice the age of Ike and Tepaha. He was thus, by the standards of the time, an old man, just as Ike and Tepaha were regarded as standing on the verge of middle-age. Yet Geronimo carried the years of his hard life well, being lean and wiry of body, and his expression was not so much savage as sardonically amused. He chose to ignore Ike, addressing himself instead to Tepaha in a tone of musing wonderment.

'And what have we here?' he inquired. 'What is this strange creature who appears to be Indian, an Apache, no less, yet who is obviously a white man's dog, licking at his master's ass and balls lest he be struck with a small stick?'

'You smell your own breath, old man,' Tepaha told him haughtily. 'To one who feeds on dog shit, all others are dogs.'

A lance-point jabbed him reprovingly. Tepaha's darting hand caught it at the haft, snapping it off with one seemingly effortless movement of his wrist. It was a tremendous feat of strength. Geronimo rewarded it by shaking his head at the brave who was about to club Tepaha.

'So,' Geronimo said, 'perhaps you are not a dog. Perhaps. So you will explain your presence with this white man, and you will tell us who he is and what he is if not your master.'

Tepaha said proudly that Ike was his friend and brother. They had been so almost before manhood, since the time when they were both prisoners in a Mexican jail under sentence of death as *bandidos*. They had broken jail together, Tepaha becoming seriously wounded as they escaped. And Ike had gotten him to a *ranchero* across the Rio Grande. The owner of the ranch, a Spanish grandee, had offered them sanctuary, then treacherously sent one of his Aztec *peons* to summon the *carbineros*. The man had reported to Ike instead, so Ike had slain the Spaniard, and as soon as Tepaha was well enough to travel, they had burned the *ranchero* buildings, and driven off the livestock; and those *peons* who cared to do so were allowed to come with them.

'We settled well back from the *Rio*,' Tepaha continued, 'in a valley some two hundred miles distant. We built a lodge there, and outbuildings. But there were many Apache in the area, and the *peons* soon left us in fear, having been slaves so long they had lost the will to fight. I would have fought, of course, Old Ike being my friend and brother. But Ike said it was not necessary. Instead, he went unarmed amongst the Apaches, and he called them brother, and he told them that they were to come to his lodge as guests and take whatever they needed. And—'

'And' – Geronimo's eyes gleamed with ironic appreciation. 'And so they came, eh? As guests. And being such, they did not rob him of his all and kill him as they otherwise would have.'

'Why should they?' Tepaha frowned. 'Do Apaches abuse friendship? Do they mistreat a brother? Or perhaps,' he added insinuatingly, 'such is the custom of the Oklahoma Apache.'

'You,' Geronimo advised him, 'are very close to death, O, Tepaha. You will be wise to offer no insults, and to answer questions, not ask them. Even now there is an Osage prisoner in this camp whose big mouth and small brain will cost him his life in the morning.'

Tepaha drew himself erect, and emitted a scornful, 'Ho! Heed me, O, Geronimo,' he continued. 'This is Old Ike King! When he shits, great mountain ranges are formed of his turds, and fearful floods are caused by his pissing, and when he farts whole deserts are blown into the sky. This I have seen. I, his chief *vaquero*. And following us come three hundred more Apache braves, *vaqueros* like myself, and their families. All are sworn brothers of Old Ike, all enemies of his enemies. So do not threaten us with the fate of your miserable Osage, for you are tempting fate even to speak of Osages and my brother, Old Ike, in the same breath!'

The other old men in the lodge exchanged secretively approving glances; for this was good talk.

But Geronimo was not easily impressed.

'You talk great shit, Apache dog,' he said. 'Nothing follows you but your shriveled asses, unless it is the *carbineros* who have chased you out of *Tejas*.'

Tepaha promised that he would soon see for himself. 'No one runs Old Ike anywhere. Neither the *carbineros* nor the *soldados* of Maximilian, nor anyone else. Old Ike has a friend, Sam Houston. Our presence in *Tejas* is an embarrassment to him, so we leave at his request.'

'And you think to establish a *ranchero* here? The bluecoats will never allow it!'

'You do not know Old Ike,' Tepaha said. 'He has a way with *soldados*. He will smile and burden them with gifts. He will agree to do as they say; and even make motions of so doing. When he does not do so, and the *soldados* return, he will again smile and give them gifts and agree to their will. Yet still he will stay where he is. They will become firm with him. Still smiling, Ike will become firm with them, but never in a way to be detected. Bullets will come out of nowhere to find their hearts, and their horses will be hamstrung and their lodges will catch fire. So after a time, the *soldados* will go hence and return no more, realizing that what cannot be changed must be accepted. This I have seen.'

Geronimo said he had seen shit, too, and also smelled it. 'This is a god?' he jeered, jerking his head at Ike. 'You will be telling us next that he can cure the pox!'

'Even so,' Tepaha said. 'Look you, old man!'

He bared his left wrist, extended it into the dim light from the fire. There was a minute patch of smallpox pits on the wrist – but only there. The deadly pox, the chronic scourge of the red men, had merely touched his flesh and gone away.

The old men were wordless with astonishment. Geronimo raised his eyes wonderingly, the sardonic expression wiped from his face.

'How?' He stared at Tepaha. 'How could this be?'

'Magic. How else?'

'Obviously. But what kind of magic?'

'With magic that only Old Ike can perform. First he casts a spell over a cow – a *cow*, yes – and the blood of that cow becomes flecked with gold. Then he takes those flecks, and smears them into the blood of the person who has been exposed to the pox. The disease tastes the blood of that person, and flees in terror, leaving only the smallest mark of its bite.'

'And it is always the same? The victim is always cured?'

'Certainly not,' Tepaha said loftily. 'Evil men, including those who are Ike's enemies, die in itching torment.'

Geronimo stood up and took Ike's hand. 'Old Ike King,' he said, 'you and Tepaha are welcome at my fire, and we will eat and drink together, and I, Geronimo, will call you brother.'

The food was *pashofa*, a kind of gruel made of hominy. Flavored with nettles, it seemed quite tasty to Ike. Yet it was somewhat on the watery side, cooked without so much as a small snake to give it body. And Tepaha, still smarting under Geronimo's recent insults, made hideous faces of displeasure as he ate.

The potent brew served them was also a corn product. When the corn was green, squaws chewed it from the cob and spat their chewings into a large pot. To this – the rough equivalent of a distiller's mash – water was added, and after a certain number of skimmings the pot was sealed, and the contents allowed to ferment.

It was very powerful stuff. As with the food, Ike found it reasonably tasty. Tepaha, of course, did not – or, at least, he appeared not to.

Such a drink, he declared loudly, would never have been served in the lodge of Old Ike King. The most humble beverage a guest might drink in Old Ike's lodge was *mescal* or *tequila*, and for honored guests – the equals of Ike and himself – there was real whiskey.

The old men around the fire squirmed in shame, and Geronimo murmured embarrassed apologies. Still, despite a reproving frown from Ike, Tepaha would not desist.

'In the lodge of Old Ike King,' Tepaha said, 'there is always meat. A guest may always fill his belly with good fat beef, and take as much with him as he will on departing. Mush is fed only to papooses, and toothless old dogs.'

'I am sorry,' Geronimo murmured. 'It has been a bad winter. There is no meat in camp.'

'Very bad planning,' Tepaha said reprovingly. 'Such could never happen with Old Ike King.'

'Sorry,' Geronimo repeated stiffly. 'If there was meat, you would be more than welcome to it.'

Tepaha gave him a jeering stare. He said he was beginning to understand Geronimo's reputation for craftiness.

'Yes, now it is clear to me. You save your meat for yourselves, and serve mush to your guests.'

It was the most terrible insult of all. For a moment, Tepaha thought that he might have gone too far. Then, at last Geronimo smiled enigmatically and stood up.

Leaving the tent, he went out into the blizzard, returning after a few moments to announce that meat was indeed available. Not enough for his entire village, but an amount more than adequate for his honored guests.

'And you and Old Ike King shall have it all, O, Tepaha. My people and I will not eat as much as a single bite.'

. . . So that was when it had happened, Ike thought. That was how it had come about that he and Tepaha had been fed the Osage prisoner.

'Why, that old son-of-a-bitch!' he bellowed, his voice echoing through the hotel's bar room. 'God damn you to hell, Tepaha—'

'Osage good eating,' Tepaha patted his stomach. 'All Osage good for, eat and screw.'

Then, the doors of the hotel lobby rolled open, and Arlie and Boz entered with their wives.

d

The two young men were dressed in approximately the same fashion as their father, even to the long knives in their boot-tops. Their squaws, each of whom took up a position behind her husband, wore levis, brightly colored flannel shirts, and buckskin moccasins and jackets.

Joshie was not quite a year older than her sister, Kay, and except for a somewhat more serious expression – a reflection of her life with Boz – might have passed as Kay's twin. Both girls had small full bodies, and were virtually the same height. Both wore their hair long, and so tightly braided as to tauten their faces, giving them a perpetually wide-eyed expression.

As their grandfather stared at them sternly, watchful for any error in deportment, the girls kept their eyes demurely downcast, their lips firmed to erase any semblance of giggling. Satisfied with his inspection, Tepaha rolled open the doors to the dining room and curtly beckoned to his grandson, I.K.

I.K. came in, hands jammed into the pockets of his mail-order suit, his bright yellow shoes tapping the floor in a kind of jaunty swagger. His brightly greased hair was parted in the middle, in the dudish fashion of the day. Despite the ominous air of the bar room, he was smiling. For he could not really believe that anything truly bad would happen to him.

He was Tepaha's youngest grandchild, and Old Ike's favorite. Both had pampered him, laughing at his fop's dress and mannerisms, only scolding him mildly for laziness and general no-accountness. So why, then, should they suddenly turn severe?

'Hi'ya, Gran'pa, Uncle Ike,' he said. 'How's your hammer hangin'?'

'Silence,' Tepaha said. 'You are in great disgrace.'

'Me? Aw, now, Gran'pa—'

Tepaha suddenly slapped him. As I.K. let out a pained howl, Tepaha slapped him again. The youth clenched his teeth, his eyes tear-filled. Tepaha drew the gleaming knife from his boot-top and handed it to him.

'You will hand this to your Uncle Ike. He will use my knife and his hand. So we both punish you for stealing from him.'

'*N-No!*' I.K. gasped. 'I – w-what is he gonna—?'

'He will cut off one of your fingers.'

'Cut off my—? *Oh, no!* P-Please, Gran'pa. Please, d-don't—'

Tepaha stared at him stonily. Implacably, he repeated his order. One finger would be cut off now. Two, if he delayed. Three if he delayed longer.

'Aw, now, looky,' Arlie protested. 'This ain't really fair.'

'Silence,' said Tepaha.

'But it ain't fair, Grandfather Tepaha. You an' Paw taught I.K. all the orneriness he knows. You laughed about his stealing. It ain't his fault—'

'Silence! He stole from his own family, your father. A great crime, and a shame to me.'

'But, dang it—!'

Tepaha swung his hand swiftly, slapping Arlie full in the face. Now, he declared, Arlie had best remain silent or he would be slapped again. Boz laughed at his brother's discomfiture.

'Boy, are you gutless! Catch me lettin' him slap *me* around!'

Arlie ignored the jibe. Tepaha grabbed his grandson by the arm, and hauled him before Old Ike. Trembling, I.K. held out his left hand, and Ike neatly sliced off his third finger and handed it back to him.

I.K. clutched it dully, holding the bleeding stump against his chest. Vacant-eyed, numb with shock, he listened as Tepaha pronounced the remainder of his sentence. He was to leave King's Junction at once. If he ever returned, he would be killed.

'Now, go,' Tepaha said, pointing. And I.K. went. And the old Apache rolled the dining room doors shut behind him.

Tepaha turned around again. His eyes found Ike's, and Ike slowly nodded; jerked his head at Boz.

'Stretch yourself out there on the floor,' he said. 'Your Gran'father Tepaha is gonna kick you.'

'*Huh?*' Boz grunted. 'What the hell you talkin' about?'

'I said to lay yourself down! Now, do it or I'll lay you!'

'B-But – but—' Boz's eyes darted nervously from his father to Tepaha. 'What the shit is this? Why is Tepaha a-wantin' to kick me?'

Ike said that the kicking was his own idea, just as cutting off I.K.'s finger had been Tepaha's. 'You kicked Joshie, his kinswoman. Now, he will kick you.'

'But, God dammit—!' Boz whirled on his wife. 'You've been lyin' about me, ain't you? Now, by Chirst, you take it back or I'll—'

'She didn't say nothin',' Arlie said idly. 'Got too much pride to admit that her own husband would kick her.'

'And I didn't, by God! Anyone that says I did is a fucking liar!'

'I said it,' Arlie grinned, 'an' I wasn't lying. So you better hump your ass for that kickin'!'

Boz dived for him, his hand darting toward his boot-top. At virtually the same instant, he found the point of Arlie's knife pricking at his throat.

'Now, you lay down, boy,' Arlie said softly. 'Get yourself down on them planks, or you're gonna be minus an Adam's apple.'

Boz lay down, cursing, vowing to get his brother if it took him a hundred years. Arlie laughed that it would take him that long to get a hard-on.

'Enough!' Old Ike growled; and to Tepaha, 'Whenever you are ready, old friend.'

Tepaha stepped forward. He kicked Boz twice, the second kick causing the young man to break wind noisily.

Arlie roared with laughter, as Boz sat up. 'Always figured you was full of shit. Reckon there ain't no doubt about it, now!'

His face white with pain and fury, Boz came slowly to his feet. Casually, Arlie turned his back on him, as though to address his wife.

It was a trap, of course. But Boz saw it as opportunity. He sprang, knife drawn. But Arlie was suddenly no longer where he had been, and, as suddenly, Boz was no longer period.

He was back on the floor again, slit from crotch to breastbone, his guts spilled out on the time-stained planks.

Arlie wiped the blood from his knife, giving his father an ostensibly mournful glance. 'I had to do it, Paw. Just wasn't no way out.'

Old Ike nodded, his face expressionless. 'I saw,' he said.

CHAPTER FOUR

a

Critchfield King stood on the open platform of the chair-car, watching the gradual pre-dawn lightening of the prairie, nervously flinging his cheroot away from him as he waited for the woman, the supposed soldier's bride.

What the hell had happened, he wondered savagely. What in God's name could be holding her up?

She had missed the money-belt immediately after their love-making, and promptly demanded its return. Teasingly, he had promised to give it back, but only if she joined him on the platform for a few kisses. She had agreed to do so, as soon as she had visited the toilet. That had been more than thirty minutes ago; considerably more, for the train had stopped at two villages since then. Soon it would be broad daylight, too late for a showdown with her without attracting fatal attention to himself. If she didn't show up within another five minutes—

She didn't. Nerves jumping, Critch feverishly sought an answer to the riddle, and quickly settled upon two.

She had sought out the conductor, and told him of the theft – the embarrassing and compromising fact that she, a married woman, had given herself to a man and been robbed in the process. It didn't seem likely that she would have been desperate or stupid

65

enough to do so, but she *might* have. In which case, he, Critch King, was in very serious trouble.

On the other hand – and this seemed more likely – something had happened to delay her in the toilet. She had taken sick, or her clothes had become conspicuously soiled by their love-making and had to be cleaned, or – Or?

He had to find out. He had nothing to lose by learning the truth. So bracing himself, putting on an air of easy self-assurance, he left the platform and went back inside the car.

Kerosene lanterns burned at either end of it, rocking and swaying with the motion of the train, dimly illuminating its dozing cargo of humanity. Seeping through the grimy windows, dawn provided more light. So, well before reaching the seat where he and the girl had been sitting, Critch could see that it was unoccupied.

He went on through the car, and into the next one, and so on through the remaining three cars of the train. He retraced his steps, pausing once to display his ticket to a yawning conductor. The man showed no interest in him whatsoever, and, breathing easier, Critch returned to his own car and the platform where he had been standing.

Still no sign of her. Cautiously, Critch reentered the car and gently tested the door of the women's toilet.

There was no response for a moment. Then, with a dull rattle of metal, it swung open. The lock had been broken. Glass, from the shattered window, covered the floor. Critch took a startled glance at the scene. Then, swiftly pulling the door to, he entered the opposite door to the men's toilet.

He locked it, stood leaning against it. Cursed

softly, as he pondered this new riddle.

The woman had jumped the train, apparently. Or, in view of the broken lock, she had been forced to jump it. Someone had broken in on her, and to escape that someone she had smashed the window glass and made her escape.

The train had stopped twice since he had last seen her. As it slowed for those stops, she could have jumped without serious risk to herself. As, also, could the person who had broken in on her, and from whom she was obviously fleeing.

But why – what—?

There could be only one answer. Someone else had known about the money belt which now rested around his middle. It hadn't belonged to the woman he had taken it from – else she would have cried out for help instead of jumping the train. Also, axiomatically, it hadn't belonged to the person who had driven her from the train (and doubtless pursued her out of the window), or that person would have sought to recover it legally. But one thing *was* a cinch!

He, Critch King, had stumbled onto something big. *Very big!* Only for very high stakes would the pursued woman and her pursuer have gone to such lengths as they had.

Critch undid the belt, dipped into its pockets for the first time. His hand jerked with surprise at the first sheaf of bills he produced, almost dropping them into the open toilet. Excitedly, he drew out another sheaf, and another, making a rough count as he did so. By the time he had emptied all the belt's pockets, his heart was pounding as it had never pounded before, and he was faint with the shock of his discovery.

He lowered the toilet seat, sat down on it. He

heard the conductor's muted bellow of *'King's Junction,'* and the train slowed and stopped, and went on again.

Critch recounted the money, distributing it sheaf by sheaf in the cunningly constructed pockets of his suit. The tailor who specialized in such clothing had boasted that a fortune could be concealed in the suit without the slightest telltale bulge. Standing up and critically examining himself, Critch saw that the tailor had made no idle brag.

Seventy-two thousand dollars – *seventy-two thousand dollars.* Yet no one would have guessed that he was hiding as much as a dollar shinplaster. He had stolen a couple of hundred dollars out of the woman's purse, so all together—

Seventy-two thousand! It was more money than he had ever dreamed of having. It was, in fact, too damned *much* money to show up with at his father's household. Even with Old Ike's very liberal views about the acquisition of money, it was far too much, particularly since most of it was in five-hundred and thousand-dollar bills. The old man would simply declare him a murderer, or at best a large-scale bank-robber, and summon a Federal marshal. And a hell of a lot of good it would do Critch King, even if he could make anyone believe the truth as to how he had come by the swag.

It was one of those cases where a lie wouldn't help and the truth was damning. If nothing worse, he would be disowned by Old Ike, disqualified for any share in his father's fortune. Obviously, then, his possession of so much money would have to be kept secret. And that being the case . . .

A plan began to form in his mind. The first step in

68

that plan was leaving the train at the boom city of El Reno, and then— Or, no, that wasn't quite the first step. Right at the moment, there was the money belt to be got rid of.

Critch tried to raise the glazed window. It was stuck, of course; the damned things were always stuck. Critch hesitated, then raised the lid of the toilet.

It was not truly a toilet, in the modern sense of the word. Merely a privy, which opened directly onto the roadbed. Critch dropped the belt into it. Then, after an approving glance at himself in the mirror, he lighted another cheroot and stepped out into the corridor.

The conductor was surveying the disarray of the women's restroom. He turned, his eyes sharpening with suspicion, as Critch came into the areaway.

'What's your name, mister?' he demanded.

'My name?' Critch considered the question, taking a thoughtful draw on his cigar. 'I don't believe,' he said coolly, 'that that is any of your God damned business.'

'Maybe I'll make it my business! Where you been sittin' tonight?'

'All over your filthy train,' Critch said, 'trying to find a seatmate who didn't stink or snore. Regrettably, I found no one who didn't do both.'

'You was settin' next to a young woman, wasn't you? For part of the night, anyways. I know you was!'

'Indeed?' Critch flicked ashes from his cheroot. 'Now, let me tell you something *I* know. That unless I am immediately provided with the drawing-room I was promised by your Tulsa ticket agent, you are going to find yourself out of a job.'

'Drawing roo— *huh?*' The conductor blinked stupidly. 'Now, looky, here—'

'Drawing room,' Critch repeated firmly. 'This train carries one car for first-class passengers, so I know you must have a drawing-room available by now. You will get my luggage out of the baggage car and take me to it, instantly.'

He extended his baggage checks, loftily holding out a five dollar bill with them. 'Your tip,' he explained. 'Well? What are you waiting for, man? I want to get cleaned up before we arrive in King's Junction.'

The conductor took the checks and the money, his dull face registering confusion. Then, in sudden alarm, he tried to thrust them back at Critch.

'*King's Junction?*' he said. 'Mister, we passed King's Junction fifteen-twenty minutes ago!'

'You *passed* it!' Critch said with a fine show of incredulity. 'After all my instructions to your man in Tulsa, you carried me past the Junction!'

'B-But – but I called it out. Maybe you didn't hear me, but—'

'I left instructions that I be called personally! Incidentally, King is the name. Critchfield King.'

'But no one told me nothin' about – *King?*' said the conductor. 'Did you say – are you any relation to – to—'

'I am. Isaac Joshua King is my father. You've heard the name, I imagine?'

The conductor nodded miserably. Had he *ever* heard of him! Everyone connected with the railroad, from president to porter, had heard of Old Ike King and dreaded incurring his wrath. Not so long before, when the railroad had been somewhat slow in paying

70

for a couple of runover cows, Old Ike had had a train log-chained to its tracks; delaying it some six hours until a division superintendent could arrive by special train to apologize and make a payment in person.

Ike King was a law unto himself. As the personal friend of at least one president of the United States – a man who had visited the Junction and hunted with him – the laws governing ordinary mortals seemed simply not to apply to him.

So now the conductor cringed and mumbled repeated apologies as Critch berated him. Never guessing the young man's real reason for the tirade. Forgetting his suspicions, the mystery of the shattered window and the missing woman, as Critch mercilessly bawled him out.

'—a disgrace. This railroad and everyone connected with it! Talk about your slow trains through Arkansas! I could have crawled faster than this thing travels!'

'Well, y'see, this is a local, Mr. King. Has to stop at every wide place in the road. Now we got an express that—'

'I'll bet! Probably has a top speed of twelve miles an hour!'

'No, sir. It can hit twenty-twenty-five, if the grade's right. But—'

'Oh, forget it. Who cares?' said Critch, with exaggerated weariness. 'You've carried me past my stop. Now, I assume you're going to tell me that you don't have a drawing room available.'

The conductor nodded unhappily. 'Did have one until a little spell ago. If I'd known—' He broke off, beaming with sudden delight. 'Your brother! Now how the heck could I have forgot?'

'My brother?' Critch frowned. 'What about him?'

'I mean, he's the one that got the last stateroom! You can share it with him!'

b

Arlie greeted Critch enthusiastically, enveloping him in a bearhug which the latter could have well done without in view of the money he was carrying. At last releasing himself, Critch shot a questioning glance at the young Indian who lolled on one of the room's upholstered benches – an Apache youth with a bandaged hand and citified clothes. Arlie said that they could talk openly, since the young man knew barely a dozen words of English.

'Gonna make it damned hard for him in El Reno,' he added. 'But he had to have a fling at city life, so Paw told him to take off.'

'I see,' Critch smiled, and he attempted to introduce himself. But through lack of usage, the Apache language had become virtually so much Greek to him. And it was left to Arlie to perform the introductions. He did so at some length, the youth apparently being rather stupid and having to ask numerous questions. Finally, however, the Indian grunted in understanding, and grinned a hopeful question at Critch.

'Whiskey?' he said.

'Why, yes,' Critch smiled. 'I have a—'

'But he ain't getting it,' Arlie declared. 'The son-of-a-bitch ain't gettin' no more until we hit El Reno. Hear me, I.K.' – he spat out another fluent stream of Apache. 'No more.'

The youth subsided, sulking with displeasure. Arlie turned his attention back to his brother, raining

72

question after question upon him, his last question, significantly, being a casual inquiry about their mother.

Critch replied that he hadn't seen her for years, and that he had no pleasant memories of her. 'I'd rather not talk about her, if you don't mind, Arlie. The past is past, and there's no point in looking back. I've managed to do very well, in spite of everything.'

'A fool could see that,' Arlie smiled warmly. 'Paw'll be plumb proud of you. How come you didn't get off at King's Junction, anyways?'

'We-el—' Critch pursed his lips judiciously. 'I had considered it. But I wasn't sure of my welcome, and I saw no reason to go home aside from the sentimental ones.'

'No reason!' Arlie exclaimed. 'Heirin' big in Paw's will wasn't a reason?'

Critch assumed an air of puzzlement, asserting that Old Ike could surely have little or nothing for his sons to inherit.

'Now, I did run into an Osage lawyer over in Tulsa – he appeared to be a pretty good fellow, at first—'

'He wrote Paw about you,' Arlie chuckled. 'Claimed you stole his wallet.'

'A real shyster,' Critch nodded equably. 'First, he stuck me for almost twenty dollars worth of drinks. Then, he showed up at my hotel the next morning and threatened to make a bad report on me if I didn't pay him five hundred. I told him I didn't care what he did, since I knew that my father was a relatively poor man.'

'*Paw, poor?* He's got some debts sure, but how come you figured he was poor?'

'Well, he never really owned any land. He had

some under lease in the Strip, but most of it he just moved in on, and took.'

'An' he's still got it, too, little brother! Got just what he always had. Them land-openings didn't change a thing with Paw.'

Critch shook his head wonderingly. 'But how in the world . . . ?'

'Let me tell you,' Arlie grinned, and he did so; relating a tale that was already familiar throughout much of the Southwest.

Arlie, Boz and Old Ike had all used their right to stake out homesteads of one-hundred-and-sixty acres. In addition, some fifth of Ike's lighter-skinned Apache followers wearing city clothes had staked out claims of similar size. Like the Kings, however, they had not made the Run, the race for homesteads, but had 'soonered' the land, putting their stakes down on territory which Old Ike had held from the start.

'You know what I mean, Critch? You savvy "sooner"?'

Critch nodded his understanding. A sooner was a person who slipped across the border ahead of the starter's gun. In years to come, it was to become an affectionate second-name for Oklahoma – that is, 'the Sooner state' – as was Jayhawk to become a nickname for Kansas and Cornhusker for Nebraska.

'O' course,' Arlie continued, 'there was a lot of fuss about it. But I reckon you know it'd take more'n fuss to move Paw, an' lucky for him he had the political pull to ride the storm through.'

'Good for him,' Critch murmured. 'But you've only accounted for a few thousand acres, Arlie. How did he recover the rest of his holdings?'

'With money,' Arlie shrugged. 'I mean, he bought up the homesteaders' claims. A lot of 'em didn't have the money to carry them through a bad year, an' had to sell to Paw. The others – well, they got kind of nervous with so many Indians livin' around 'em. Got the idea, somehow, that their scalps might wind up on a pole if they didn't sell. So—'

'I see,' Critch said. 'I think I get the picture.'

'Now, don't get no wrong ideas,' his brother protested. 'Maybe they had a leetle pressure put on 'em, but they all got a fair price for their claims. More'n they were worth in most cases. You wouldn't remember, bein' away so long, but a heap of the land out here just ain't fit for nothing but grazin'. Try to put a plow to it, an it'll blow away on you. Frankly' – he shook his head, troubledly, 'I wish Paw didn't have so danged much land. Wish we had less land, and more money to work it with. I tell you, Critch, I get so damned worried at times that . . .'

He shook his head again, his voice trailing off into silence. Then, his expression clearing, he said, well, to hell with it.

'You and me'll work things out together, little brother. I couldn't do anything with that God damned Boz, but now that I got him out of the way . . .'

'Uh – out of the way?' Critch said.

'I killed the son-of-a-bitch. Prodded him in to makin' a try for me, and then I gutted him. I just had to do it, Critch. He'd've got me if I hadn't. There was a couple of times when the bastard would've killed me if I hadn't been watching sharp.'

'That sounds like Boz, all right,' Critch nodded. 'He was always mean and sneaky.' And he silently added to himself that the manner of Boz's death was also typical of Arlie. Boz had bitten off far more than he could chew in tying into the middle-brother.

Despite Arlie's open countenance and bubbling good humor, he could be deadly hard when he had to be. More importantly, he was smart enough to get away with the results of his hardness – transferring the bee from his own back to his victim's.

As the train poked along through the prairie, Critch nodded and smiled as Arlie rambled on genially. Nodded and smiled without actually listening, slowly coming to a decision in his own mind.

He wasn't going back to King's Junction. With seventy-two thousand dollars in his poke, he didn't need to go back. It was sufficient to support him in luxury to a ripe old age, so he could do quite well without his inheritance from Old Ike. In fact, as Arlie painted the picture, the inheritance was more potential than actual. The King holdings were burdened with debt, and Ike's feudal manner of doing things made that debt doubly burdensome. He, Critch, could easily be a very old man before his potential wealth became a reality. And it was highly unlikely that Arlie would allow him to live to be an old man.

Arlie appeared to like him, and doubtless did. Still, he would regard Critch as a threat – just as he had regarded Boz as one. So . . .

He'd be on his home ground, Critch thought. Home for him, and strange territory for me. I don't buck another man's game; I was a sucker to even think of it. Mr. Critchfield King will settle for what he's got, and stay healthy!

At El Reno, Arlie dismissed the Indian youth with a few silver dollars and a guttural torrent of Apache. Then, grabbing up Critch's bags with his own, he tossed them onto the dray of the town's leading hotel.

'We'll register-in later,' he told his brother. 'Right

now, we got to get over to the U.S. Marshal's office.'

'Marshal's office?' Critch blinked. 'What for?'

'So's I can report that little accident that happened to Boz, like I came here to do,' Arlie said. 'What's the matter with you, boy? Ain't you been listenin' to nothing I said?'

'Well, uh – But I've got some business to take care of, Arlie. Suppose I get it out of the way while you see the marshal, and we can—'

'Suppose,' Arlie cut in, 'you come along to the marshal's office with me like you already promised to do. Sort of give me your moral support, as the sayin' is.'

'But – but it's very important that I—'

'Might not be,' Arlie said firmly. 'No, sir, it might turn out a hell of a lot more important for you t'be introduced proper to the marshal. There's a flock of sharpers and high-binders floddin' into El Reno, and a dude-lookin' fella like you could get mistook for one of 'em. Yes, sir,' he added slowly, 'you could get mistook awfully easy, Critch. Wouldn't be at all surprised if you was picked up an' shook down before you'd gone a quarter-mile.'

Critch gave him a sharp look. But if there was a double meaning in his brother's words, a threat, there was nothing to indicate the fact in the latter's expression. Rather, Arlie seemed genuinely concerned for his welfare, anxious that his younger kinsman should get off on the right foot in these new surroundings.

So Critch smiled pleasantly, and told Arlie to lead the way. 'The marshal's office,' he said. 'I'll take care of my business later.'

El Reno, the site of the Federal land lottery, rose from the prairie in a conglomerate mass of solid brick and rickety frame buildings, some of one-story and false front, others three or four floors in height; for this was both an old town, as time was measured in the Territory, and a new one. There were even some 'tent buildings' – structures made of canvas stretched over a framework of wood. And sprawling out over the gently rolling grassland, for almost as far as the eye could see, was a chaotic array of tents and shacks thrown up by the newcome settlers.

The dusty streets were choked with covered wagons and drays and buggies, through which saddle-worn horsemen patiently wended their weary way. Most of these last were out-of-work cowhands, uprooted and unwanted as the plough furrowed through their one-time domain of the Cherokee Strip, the Big Pasture and other Territorial lands. Some might still find jobs in Texas, or westward in the states-to-be of Wyoming and New Mexico. (Or perhaps as far north as North-western Nebraska and the Dakotas.) A few, out of hateful necessity, would manage to make the transformation from cowboy to clodhopper. Some would turn outlaw. Some would become peace officers, hunting down the very men they had once worked with and called friend. As for the remainder . . . well, who knew? What *does* happen to men who can find no other path for themselves than the one occupied by the juggernaut of an onrushing civilization? To quote from the sardonic philosophy of the times, they were caught ziggin' when they shoulda been zaggin'. They had played the red, and the black came up.

The sidewalks, which were even more jammed than the streets, were of plank and of various levels, according to the whim of the owner of the business establishment upon which they fronted. If he chose to have a porch, the walk rose by steps to become part of it; descending at the porch's end to the entrance level of the adjoining establishment.

'God damn,' said Arlie exultantly, as he lunged through the crowds. 'Didja ever see anything like this, little brother?'

'Like it,' Critch said a little breathlessly. 'But not so much of it.'

'A real piss-walloper, ain't she? A rip-roarin' son-of-a-bitch!'

'If it isn't,' Critch replied, 'it'll do until one comes along.'

Blanket Indians sat with their backs against building fronts, their legs innocently thrust straight out in front of them for the unwary passer-by to trip over. Sunbonneted, gingham clad settlers' wives rubbed shoulders with skimpily-dressed saloon girls. Cowboys brushed against clodhoppers. Indians, merchants, gamblers, drummers (*salesmen*), clerks, workmen, women of all ages and descriptions; the bountiful, the beautiful, the damned – all were jam-packed together in a chaotic, colorful mass.

Drifting out through innumerable swinging-doors, came the aroma of beer, booze and free-lunch, and the muted roar of many sounds. The click of roulette wheels, the rattle of gambling chips; the tinny tinkling of pianos, boisterous shouts and laughter, feminine squeals of protest.

Despite the devil-may-care air of things, the free-and-easy atmosphere, there was no sound of gunplay, no sign of brawling. For El Reno was very well

79

policed – as Critch was soon to discover.

It happened as he was passing a saloon, trailing Arlie by a step or two. There was a sudden explosion of yells and curses, the scraping clatter of shattering wood. The whole building seemed to tremble with it. And then out through the swinging doors burst a mass of men, their rush carrying them out into the street and slamming Critch against a hitching post.

Apparently, they had done nothing serious – merely brawled, perhaps – for the two deputy marshals who followed them into the street dismissed them after administering a few judiciously vigorous shakes and slaps. Shaken and furious, Critch picked up his dust-smeared hat; straightened to find himself looking into a pair of amiable but steely eyes.

'Nice day,' the man greeted him pleasantly. 'Mind telling me who you are, mister?'

'You're God damned right I mind!' Critch snarled. 'Who the hell are you?'

'Name's Tilghman, Bill Tilghman.'

The name didn't immediately register on Critch; the fact that this was one of the West's most famous peace officers. He made a profanely filthy suggestion to the man – or rather he started to. The first word or so was barely out of his mouth, when the cold muzzle of a .45 jabbed into his stomach.

'Now, reach!' the officer said. 'Get those hands up!'

Critch got them up, looking around wildly for Arlie. They had become separated in the fracas, and now he could see him nowhere.

The two deputy marshals came back from the street; looked interestedly at Critch. 'What you got here, Bill?'

'Someone with some pretty bad manners, for one thing. Let's see what else he's got.'

'Sure thing.'

The two deputies moved in for a search. Then, just as one stopped to feel Critch's trousers and the other yanked his coat open . . .

'Hey, there, you fellas! What you doin' to my little brother?'

Arlie pushed through the crowd, dropped a protective arm around his shoulders. Almost faint with relief, Critch heard him say that, sure, this was his brother. Been away from home since he was a kid, but now he was comin' back to stay.

'Mr. Tilghman, this here is—'

'We've met,' Tilghman said, and he turned on his heel and walked away. Critch was introduced to the other two men, Deputy Marshals Heck Thomas and Chris Madsen, who returned his nervously effusive greetings with dry amusement.

'Well, let's see, now,' Arlie said. 'That's about all you fellas, ain't it? No one else that might take Critch for somethin' that he ain't?'

'There's still Jim,' Madsen said. 'He was headin' for the marshal's office the last I saw.'

'Good,' Arlie said. 'That's right where we're goin'.'

As they went on their way, he good-naturedly cursed Critch, inquiring how he had ever managed to live so long with such ostensibly offensive manners; shaking his head to Critch's explanation that the bad jolting he had gotten had caused him to lose his temper.

'Better watch where you lose it from now on, boy,' he said, and Critch meekly promised that he would.

They reached the Federal building, ascended to

the marshal's headquarters on the second floor. In the outer office, a heavy-set young man with the profile of McKinley was laboriously filling out a warrant on a rickety typewriter. Arlie introduced him as Deputy Marshal Jim Thompson.

'Ol' Jim used t'be a school-teacher, Critch. His uncle Harry is the marshal here.'

'Neither fact' – Thompson shook hands, smiling, 'having anything to do with my present employment. Incidentally, my full name is James Sherman Thompson.'

'Now, don't that beat all!' Arlie exclaimed. 'Ain't hardly no one in the Territory that ain't a reb, but ol' Jim always mentions his middle name! Probably'll get him killed some day.'

'I doubt that,' said U.S. Marshal Harry Thompson. 'I doubt it very much.'

He stood in the doorway of his office, a tall distinguished looking man with coal-black hair and eyes, who bore some resemblance to the now-retired outlaw, Frank James. He was well-spoken; immaculately dressed in spotless linen and black broadcloth. For a United States Marshal is a high government offical, comparable in rank to a Federal Judge, and not the roughneck two-gun man of popular fiction.

He gave his nephew a look which sent that young man hurrying back to his typewriter, then courteously gestured the King brothers inside. He listened impassively, the tips of his fingers pressed together, as Arlie told of the killing of Boz. When Arlie had at last finished, with a nervous rush of words, the marshal remained silent for a long moment. Then, leaning forward casually, he plucked the knife from young King's boot-top.

'A genuine Bowie, isn't it?' he asked.

'Sure is, Marshal Harry. One that ol' Jim gave to Paw hisself.'

'So you told me,' the marshal nodded. 'And what did I tell you? About bringing weapons into my office, that is?'

'Gosh, Marshal Harry' – Arlie ran a nervous finger around his collar. 'I plumb forgot, honest!'

'If you forget again,' Thompson said softly, 'I'm going to be angry with you.'

He flipped the knife suddenly. It landed point down, almost scraping Arlie's booted foot, the haft quivering with the force of the throw. Arlie tugged it out of the flooring, a little pallid beneath his tan. He shoved it as deep down into his boot as he could, making it as inconspicuous as possible.

'Now,' Thompson said, 'I have no doubt that your brother's killing took place exactly as you've told me. It was self-defense. I also have no doubt, however, that it could have been avoided.'

'But the son-of-a-bitch tried t'kill me, Marshal Harry! Been tryin' t'get me for a long time!'

'Was he? Why didn't you report the fact to me?'

'Because it wouldn't've done no good! I could-n't've proved nothin'!'

'You wouldn't have had to. I'm sure a warning from me would have stopped Boz's attempts.'

'But – but, god-dang it, Marshal—!'

'Mmm-hmm. That isn't the King way of doing things, is it?'

'No, it ain't, by God!'

'But it will be from now on,' Thompson said. 'Your father is too old to change, and it's immaterial that he should at his time of life. But you, Arlie, and you too, sir' – he included Critch in his glance – 'you two must mature with this country, come of age with it, or cease to be a part of it. I mean that most sincerely, gentlemen. There will be no more taking of the law into one's own hands at King's Junction. If there is, I'll see to it that the person responsible goes to the gallows. Now, before you leave . . .'

He reached into his desk, took out a 'wanted' circular and passed it to Arlie, explaining that the woodcut pictures thereon had been drawn from descriptions of the criminals, and were probably inexact likenesses.

Arlie let out an appreciative, 'Whoeee!' as he glanced at the circular. Then, frowning with the effort, occasionally faltering over the words, he read its inscription aloud:

'Wanted for murder . . . Ten thousand dollars reward . . . Anne an' Eth, uh, Eth-el Anderson, al – alie, uh, a-lias Little Sis and Big Sis Anderson. Last seen near the town of Olathe, Kansas. Approach with caution, as subjects are known to have killed thirty—'

Arlie broke off, shaking his head in disbelief. 'Now, God damn, Marshal Harry! You ain't gonna tell me that these cute little ol' gals killed thirty people!'

'No,' Thompson agreed, 'the figure is incorrect. The bodies of seven more men have been discovered since that flyer was issued. Those two young women ran a roadhouse in Kansas. Any well-heeled male who stopped there was very apt to go no further. One of the sisters took him to bed, and the other one killed him.'

'Holy Jeez-ass! For some o' that it'd damn' near be worth it! But how come I ain't read nothin' about this in the papers?'

Marshal Thompson said that the story had been

kept out of the newspapers with their cooperation. It was believed best to let the Anderson women think they were unwanted, meanwhile circularizing inns and other establishments serving the public.

'As we piece the facts together,' he continued. 'Anne – that's the younger one – skipped out on her sister, taking their combined loot with her. Ethel – the older, smarter and harder of the two – apparently is hot on Anne's trail. So if you should encounter one, the other probably isn't far behind.'

'Well, I'll be damned! An' you figure they're here in the Territory?'

'They could be. It would hardly seem a likely place for a fugitive to head for.'

Arlie promised to be on the watch for the murderous Andersons, and handed the circular to the brother.

Critch took it – and stared.

d

Why, the bitch had been on the train with them! She'd had to be! Might even have watched while Little Sis got the bone put to her! And the minute he'd stepped out to the platform, and Little Sis had entered the toilet . . .

Ann, Little Sis, had known that her sister wouldn't listen to reason. With or without the money, Ethel was sure to kill her. So she'd jumped the train, and Big Sis had pursued her. And what had happened then . . .

'Yes, Mr. King?' said Marshal Thompson. 'Have you seen those women?'

Critch didn't answer him immediately. Nor did he look up. He was distrustful of his voice, fearful of what might be read from his expression. Not until he was in full control of himself and the marshal had spoken to him a second time, did he raise his eyes and speak.

'I'm not absolutely positive,' he said, his tone indicating a desire for absolute positiveness, 'but I think I may have seen the younger woman.'

'When and where?'

'Well . . . I'd say it had been within the last month. Just where, I have no idea. It might have been in the Dakotas, Texas, almost anywhere.'

'Texas or the Dakotas?' The marshal's brows went up. 'That's a lot of traveling for one month.'

'I enjoy travel,' Critch shrugged, 'and fortunately I can afford it.'

'Two good reasons for indulging in it,' Thompson nodded. 'Do you have a third?'

'Yes, sir. It's the only way I know of getting from one place to another.'

Arlie broke in with a nervous, 'God damn it, Critch! Don't you sass Marshal Harry!' But Thompson held up a hand, silencing him.

'You seem,' he said to Critch, 'to be somewhat on the defensive, Mr. King.'

'You seem to have put me there, sir. As a man with nothing to hide, I naturally resent it.'

'And as a man *with* something to hide, the best defense would be a strong offense.'

'Perhaps. You'd know more about that than I would, sir.'

Marshal Thompson nodded equably. Again he placed the tips of his fingers together, creakily rocking back and forth in his swivel chair. 'An attorney acquaintance of mine, a Mr. Al Jennings, once assured me that every man – during his lifetime – breaches the law sufficiently, in one way or another, to earn him a death sentence. Assuming his theory to be true' – the black eyes bored into Critch's face. 'Assuming it – which I don't – would you say that you were an exception to it?'

'Would you?'

'Happily,' the marshal said, 'theoretical issues are not for me to judge nor act upon. On the contrary, I am precluded from dealing with anything but facts. And the fact is, as we both know, that you are not wanted anywhere. Whether you should be is not the concern of the law, but your conscience.'

'My conscience is completely clear, marshal,' Critch smiled.

'Indeed? Then you must stand unique in this very naughty world of ours. But no matter. Through no fault of your own, you got off to a bad start in life. You seem to have survived it well, however, and the book is closed on those means by which you did so. You are in a new country. You are beginning a new life. Make it a good one, Mr. King. Make it a good one. Now, since you're apparently unable to tell me anything useful about the Anderson women . . .'

He stood up and held out his hand.

The King brothers shook it, Arlie edging toward the door even as he did so. And once out of the office, he hustled Critch toward the nearest saloon, fervently declaring his need for three fingers in a rain-barrel.

'God damn!' he swore, gulping down a tin cup of forty-rod. 'Don't know what there is about that fella that gets me so God damned rattled. Jus' looks at me an' I start shittin' in my pants.'

Critch laughed. 'Why, I thought he was very pleasant.'

'Yeah, you handled him just fine,' Arlie nodded.

'Had me kind of uneasy for a minute, the way you was talkin' up to him, but I reckon you knowed what you was doin'. Got to hand it to you, little brother,' he added admiringly. 'I was sure plenty glad you was with me.'

'So was I. It's always useful to know a man in his position,' Critch said. And he meant every word of it.

His meeting with the marshal had convinced him of the wisdom of steering clear of King's Junction. Or any other place within Thompson's jurisdiction. Otherwise, he would be inviting disaster upon himself. Thus far, he had been extremely lucky, staying out of jail, keeping off the wanted lists. But luck was largely a matter of weighing the odds, and the odds were all against him at King's Junction. Trouble could seek him out there, even though he did nothing culpable himself. With his shady background, of which the marshal obviously had considerable knowledge, he would become immediately suspect in the event of any wrongdong, regardless of whether he was responsible for it.

His next move, then? Well, not the one he had decided on before meeting the marshal. He had planned to have the bulk of his stolen seventy-two thousand converted into cashier's checks, doing it through a number of banks to avoid attention. Now, even that seemed risky – riskier than keeping the money on him until he could jump to Texas or Kansas or wherever the hell he had to to escape Marshal Thompson's watchful eye.

No one knew that he had such a huge sum on him. Arlie might have learned something via his several bearhugs, enough to make him suspect that Critch had a considerable amount of cash. And Arlie certainly wasn't above stealing, if he considered it safe. But there was a very simple way of protecting himself against Arlie.

He ordered another round of drinks, paid for them from a wallet still modestly fat with the contents of Anne Anderson's purse. They drank, and Critch drew confidentially close to his brother.

'Something I want to tell you, Arlie,' he said, low-voiced. 'I've got quite a bit of money on me.'

'I could see,' Arlie grinned. 'Couldn't help peekin'.'

'More than that. Several thousand dollars. Now, I'd thought about converting it into bank checks. But after all, what's the point? I can put it in Paw's safe as soon as we get to the Junction. Meanwhile, now that you know I've got it and we can both be on the look-out for pickpockets and thieves . . .'

Arlie's face sagged ludicrously. Critch almost laughed out loud. So the sneaky son-of-a-bitch had planned to steal it! And now he's had his role changed from thief to watchdog!

But not for long, Brother Arlie. Just until I jump town on you tonight.

'Well, now looky, little brother,' Arlie began uncomfortably. 'I, uh, ain't real sure that, uh—'

'You don't think it's a good idea? Well, maybe you're right. I'll just step over to the bank and buy checks with the money.'

'Well, uh . . .'

Arlie wasn't sure that that was a good idea either. Naturally stealing checks would do him no good. On the other hand, he obviously had no 'good' ideas of his own, i.e., some scheme for appropriating the prize which he had been nominated to protect.

'Well, all right,' he said, at last, his voice very grumpy. 'But dang it, Critch, you be watchin' out, yourself! That money gets stole off of you, Paw'll nail my hide to the barn door!'

'Oh, I'll be careful,' Critch promised. 'I've always believed that an ounce of prevention is worth a pound of cure.'

'You have, huh? Me, I've always believed that shit stinks.'

'Something wrong?' Critch asked innocently. 'Did I say something to offend you?'

Looking back on the moment later, he would curse himself roundly for his smugness; wondering how he could ever have forgotten that Arlie was an expert at dissembling, that the way he acted was not necessarily indicative of the way he felt. At the time, however . . .

'Shouldn't we be getting checked in at the hotel?' he suggested. 'I'd like to clean up, and get a bite to eat.'

Arlie nodded curtly, and gulped down the rest of his drink. 'Well, let's get goin'. No sense in—' He broke off frowning, then reached out and plucked at Critch's coat. 'Damned if you ain't bustin' out at the seams, boy.'

'What?'

'Looky,' Arlie pointed. 'Can't see it unless you sorta stretch your shoulders a certain way, but – Why, by damn, there's another place! An' here's another one. An' another one, an' – I never seen nothin' like it! A whole mess of little gapes at the seams, like maybe the threads had been cut.'

Critch looked; turned slowly around to examine himself in the back-bar mirror. He looked at Arlie, now frowning at him in innocent concern.

'That coat's sure one helluva mess, little brother.

You suppose maybe you could make the tailor give you your money back?'

'I hardly think so,' Critch said.

'Well, anyways, I sure hope you didn't lose no money out of all them little holes. I sure hope nothin' like that happened.'

'Now, what ever gave you that idea?' Critch said. *'You sneaky son-of-a-bitch!'*

And he suddenly slugged his brother.

That was a mistake, of course. He was simply no match for the brawny, ranch-toughened Arlie. The latter rocked with his blow, absorbing it harmlessly. Then, after a moment of ducking and dodging, of attempting to pacify Critch, he knocked him cold with a single punch.

Arlie picked him up from the floor, draped him across his shoulder. Carrying Critch's hat in his free hand, he headed toward the hotel; stopping once along the way when he was accosted by Deputy Marshal Chris Madsen. Madsen was officially curious about Critch's condition. Arlie said he just couldn't understand it himself.

'Why, we was talkin' and drinkin' just as friendly as you please, when all 't once he tried t' slug me. Called me a real dirty name, too. Hate to think I had a brother that couldn't hold his whiskey, but it sure looks that way, don't it?'

Madsen nodded drily. 'Can't have a King like that, now, can we? But I reckon you'll see to his reformin'.'

'Oh, I will, I will,' Arlie promised. 'Why, I'll bet you won't even know ol' Critch the next time you see him. No, sir, you won't even know him!'

CHAPTER FIVE

a

In the weed-grown right-of-way, Ethel (Big Sis) Anderson found a rusty shovel-blade, its handle broken off, a discard from some section-crew's tool box. With it, she scooped out a grave in the track roadbed, and buried Anne's body deep within it.

It was almost full daylight by the time she had finished. Dusting her hands, she looked around the countryside; at the rutty road on one side of the tracks, the prairie farmland on the other. She decided against the road almost immediately: she had to know *where* she was going before attempting to go anywhere. A chance to reconnoiter, to think was the first order of the day, and that meant finding a safe place to hole-up.

She leaped the right-of-way ditch, climbed over the two-strand fence. With the nearly flat terrain, she could see for several miles; and her shrewd eyes correctly interpreted what she saw. No smoke came from the chimneys of the house immediately beyond the field in which she now stood, nor was there any sign of life around the several adjacent farm buildings. But she would have known that without looking. The field, with its three-year-old wheat stubble, itself told her that the farm was abandoned.

A sandy-loam soil, repeatedly planted to the same

cereal crop. Try that for a few years, and see what happened to your farm!

Ethel and Anne Anderson had been the daughters of a farmer. He had incestuously begun their education in sex, a fact which considerably accounted for their cold-blooded treatment of men in later years. Except for sex he had taught them nothing – unless it was that greed and ignorance are pool tools for a farmer.

Year after year, he had planted the same soil-robbing crops. Ignoring the warnings in the gradually decreasing yields. Fertilizing scantily, if at all; giving the depleted land no chance for restful fallowing. And then, when the once-good earth would no longer bear, he had cursed it for the worthlessness which he himself had brought to it – and begun to cast about for still more land to ruin.

Well, he'd died happy, Ethel thought grimly. Got the hatchet in his head, right while he was pouring it on Little Sis.

Ethel had planned on going back to farming at some vague time in the future, and Anne had appeared to go along with the idea. Ethel had even decided that their farm – large, well-equipped and completely modern – would be in Oklahoma. The new land offered a good place to lose a bad past. Also, many newcomers would be carrying their fortunes with them. And currency of large denomination – the one kind which would permit a fortune to be conveniently and inconspicuously carried – would not arouse the suspicion in the Territory that it might elsewhere.

With their ultimate goal in mind, Ethel had periodically left the roadhouse for visits to various cities, where the loot which she and her sister had acquired through murder was converted into big bills. It was while she was away on one of these trips that Anne had skipped out, taking their combined swag with her.

By this time, however, following the dictates of her older sister had become second-nature with Anne. She did it unconsciously, without realizing that she was doing it. So inevitably, she had eventually headed into the Territory, just as Ethel had been sure she would. And Ethel had promptly taken note of her arrival in Tulsa – though not, as it turned out, quite promptly enough. That fancy-pants dude had gotten to Little Sis first.

Reaching the yard of the abandoned farm, Ethel drank and washed at the well, then inspected herself as best she could in her small pocket mirror.

Her face, hands and other exposed portions of her body were stained in semblance of a deep tan. Her hair was cropped short. She wore loose-fitting men's clothes – bib overalls and jumper, blue workshirt, and a battered felt hat. To all appearances, she was a casual laborer or farm hand, a role she had success-fully played for weeks. A role she would continue to play, until and unless – well, no matter. She would know when the time came.

Revealing herself as a woman was tied-in with finding a satisfactory place to hole-up – plus. A place from which she could safely go about recovering that seventy-two thousand dollars. For never for a moment did she consider not recovering it. Acquir-ing it had cost more than thirty lives, and she was ready to gamble her own life in getting it back.

Leaving the abandoned farm, she trudged off across the prairie, steering wide of any occupied farms; thinking back on the dude who had bilked Little Sis, and gotten away.

She had seen the guy somewhere before, Ethel was sure. At one time or another, they had been in the same criminal haunt at the same time, and he had been pointed out to her. Not only that but his name had been mentioned – and naturally it wasn't Crittenden, as he had told Little Sis. But it was a similar sounding name. Something like Crissfeld or Crittenwell, or . . . well, a real fancy handle. Whether it was his first name or last, she couldn't remember. But the other name (whether first or last) had been fairly common; too ordinary to stick in her memory. But if she could just bring it back, associate one name with the other . . .

And I will, Ethel confidently assured herself. I'll remember the bastard's right name in full. I'll catch up with him, and he'd better have that money when I do!

The sun was almost directly overhead when she at last found the kind of place she was looking for. One that seemingly offered not only refuge, but help as well. She studied it from a distance, a farm with well-tilled fields, and substantial outbuildings, but a house that could not possibly contain more than one room. She was too far away to tell much about the farmer, except that he was bearded and somewhat heavyset. Apparently, however, he lived alone – as he had to, for her purposes. So by noontime, after some inner debate, and after he had unhitched his team from their plough and led them into the barn, she had come to a favorable decision about him.

He was in the house eating when she appeared in the doorway, a man in his middle forties with a dull Teutonic face. He stood up, blinking at her stupidly, brushing food from his mouth with a sleeve.

'Yah?' he said. 'Vot iss, mister?'

Ethel laughed, dropping her masquerade huskiness of voice. 'Not mister, honey. You got wife, woman?'

'No got. Vy iss your business?'

'Well, now, you just have a look and see,' Ethel said.

She crossed to a corner of the room, where a strawtick resting on some nailed-together two-by-fours did duty as a bed. Casually, she removed her clothes, stood naked before him.

A glazed look had come into his eyes; a trace of spittle coursed from the corner of his mouth. But he remained cautious.

'Vy?' he said; then, 'How much?'

'No money,' Ethel smiled. 'Nothing that you can't handle.'

'Yah?'

'Yah. So come on and have a sample. I'll clear out afterwards, if you don't want me to stay.'

She stretched out on the bed, opened her arms and legs to him. The farmer – his name was Gutzman – emphatically declared, after an hour's sampling, that he wanted her to stay. He wanted her to stay forever and ever, and he would say nothing of her presence to anyone (no one ever visited him, anyway). And if her brute husband from Nebraska should come looking for her, he, Gutzman would kill him on the spot.

'Good care I take of you, little Greta,' he promised, hugging her to him. 'Vot you ask, I do.'

He meant it, although she had little to ask of him for the time being. In his attentiveness, his anxiety to please her, she became bored to the point of screaming. But she did not scream, of course, but wisely pretended to reciprocate his feelings. And tasting such wonders as he had never known, as he had believed it impossible to know, Gutzman almost sobbed in gratitude.

He had never experienced love, or even liking. Hungry for talk, he was barred from it by an inability to communicate. So always he was the mute stranger in any group, drinking in the tantalizing words of others. Always, he was the outsider, the man doomed to stand apart from those who talked and laughed. Many times he had tried to become one of them, grinning and nodding hopefully when they cast him a glance. Breathlessly wedging in on their conversation with blurted-out remarks. But his eagerness, his anxiety to please, seemed only to heighten the wall which life had built round him. People drew further away from him, leaving his statements hanging in the air unremarked. Taking little note of his existence, except for sly glances and secretive whispers.

Now, however, everything was different. His little Greta (*Ethel*) had made it so. Within her loins, he had found far more than release for his pent-up seed. In this, the ultimate gift of her body, there had been reassurance, a bolstering of his ego, an unqualified declaration of his desirability. And Hans Gutzman burst out of his shell to at last become part of life.

After a few days, he could even accept Ethel's acid-edged ribbing without feeling rebuffed. He was a little shocked by her language sometimes, but delightfully so; looking upon it as yet another naughtily charming gift from this woman of all women.

'Take it easy, Gutzy,' she would say, 'you horny old son-of-a-bitch. Those are my tits you're squeezing, not a couple of stacks of cowshit.'

'*Hee, hee!*' – a shocked giggle from Gutzman. 'You badt girl, Greta. Maybe I spank your bottom, ya?'

'Why not? You've done every other goddamn thing to it.'

'*Good* badt girl, my Greta. Maybe I saddle horses tonight. Ve take nice ride, yah?'

'Yah. Now you're talkin', Gutzy.'

The horseback rides became nightly occurrences. Sometimes they lasted for hours, Gutzman jabbering on endlessly about the places they passed and the places beyond; who lived here or there or over there. Telling her everything he knew – since she seemed greatly interested – about the various towns and villages.

So, at last, amidst the unsorted dross of his chattering, Ethel found gold. They had ridden unusually far that night, the end of her first week with him. Ethel had become very tired, and Gutzman mistook her weariness for boredom. Thus, fearful as always of losing her, he had humbly apologized for being poor company – for having so little to offer – and promised to relieve the monotony by taking her on a sightseeing trip.

'Not for more than a day it vould be, because of der animals. But ve could—'

'Oh, hell, Gutzy,' Ethel yawned. 'What's there to see around here?'

'Vell – vell, dere is, uh—'

'Yah?'

'Vell, hu—' Gutzman suddenly brightened, remembering. 'Not so far to der vest, dere is dis very fonny place. It is owned by an old man, a vite man – a beeg ranch, almost a whole county it iss, mit a little town. But dis vite man, only Indians he has to vork for him. Hundreds of vild Indians.'

'Honey,' Ethel said. 'I wouldn't walk across the street to watch an Indian screw himself in the ear.'

'Iss fonny place,' Gutzman insisted. 'Dis old vite man, badt poys, he has. Oh, dey are very mean, dis old man's sons. Already, vun of dem has killed his brother. And now anudder son has come home, so – so, uh, vell—'

'That's funny, all right,' Ethel said. 'I'm weak from laughter.'

'Iss called the Junction,' Gutzman mumbled. 'King's Junction. Der sons are—'

'King!' Ethel exclaimed, suddenly coming alive. 'Critchfield King!'

Gutzman stared at her in the moonlight. At last nodded, frowning suspiciously. 'Yah, dere is a poy named Critchfield. How you know?'

'I guessed it, you potbellied horse's ass!' Ethel laughed gaily. 'I'm the best God damned little guesser in the world.'

'But – guess you could not!'

'I just did, Gutzy. Iss so – yah?'

'No! You lie to me!'

Ethel looked at him coldly. She said, all right, if that was the way he wanted it. 'But if that *is* the way you want it, Gutzy, you've just lost a bedmate. I'm moving out on you!'

'But – but, *liebchick*. All I vant iss—'

'All you want,' Ethel said, 'is someone to screw all night, and listen to you all day, yah? And that's what I give you, yah? So if you want me to keep on giving it to you, Gutzy, you'd better pop to. When I tell you something, you'd God damned well better believe it, get me? You do it, or you'll be talking to yourself and skinning your dingus through a knothole.'

'But – but—'

'No buts. You see that thing up there in the sky? You think that's a moon? Well, it's not, Gutzy. It's a solid-gold pisspot. The angels use it whenever they have to take a leak. Iss right, yah?'

Gutzman gulped painfully. He wet his lips, looking at the soft swelling of her breasts as she breathed; at the rich thighs, suggestively spread over the saddle.

'Well?' Ethel said. 'Do you believe me or not? How about it? Are you going to have me or a knothole?'

Gutzman nodded feebly, his voice a mere whisper. 'Yah. I believe.'

'Believe what?'

'Iss – iss no moon. Only solidt-gold pisspot.'

'Good boy,' Ethel smiled approvingly. 'Now, we understand each other.'

'And now you are mine, Greta? Alvays, you vill be mine?'

'Always,' Ethel promised. 'As long as you live . . .'

b

His head buried in his hands, Critch sat on the edge of the bed in his hotel room, grimly wishing that he could bury *Arlie*'s head (preferably in cement, and after severing it from his body), if for no other reason than to stop his brother's endless sympathizing. It was bad enough to have lost the seventy-two thousand dollars. But to have to listen to the woeful mourning of the man who had stolen it from him – well, that was too damned much to bear!

Arlie had been laving him with sympathy for hours. Ever since he had carried Critch up to his room, and brought him back into consciousness. And how understanding, how forgiving, he had been over Critch's earlier attempt to slug him!

Now, don't you fret none, little brother. Mighta done the same thing myself. Fella loses a lot o' money, he just naturally strikes out at anything near him.

Critch reached down to the floor for the whiskey bottle; momentarily drowned out Arlie's voice in a long, gurgling drink. The drink emptied the bottle, and he pitched it into the wastebasket where also reposed his ruined coat.

'. . . awful lotta whiskey this afternoon.' *Arlie again, God damn him!* 'Why'n't you let me get you somethin' to eat, Critch?'

'No,' Critch said curtly. 'I'll eat when I'm ready.'

'But . . . well, all right. Reckon I'd feel the same way, in your place.' Arlie shook his head sadly. 'I sure feel sorry for you, Critch. Sure wish there was somethin' I could do for you.'

'I wish there was something I could do for *you*,' Critch said.

'Y'know,' Arlie continued in a musing tone. 'Y'know what I figure, Critch? I figure that money musta been stolen off of you after we left the marshal's office. Otherwise, Marshal Harry woulda spotted them slits in your coat, and wanted to know what was what.'

'Well? What about it?'

'Well, o' course, we did pass a lot of people between his office an' that saloon. But it does narrow things down a little, don't it? I mean, knowin' about when you was robbed. So maybe if you was t'go to Marshal Harry an' report the theft . . .'

His voice trailed off into silence, his eyes sliding away from Critch's bitter gaze. 'Well, uh, maybe,' he resumed, after a moment's silence. 'Maybe that wouldn't be such a good idea after all. Might get yourself tied up in more questionin' than you could get free of in a year o' Sundays. Ol' Harry, he'd probably want to know just how you came by the money an' why a educated fella like you was carryin' it around in cash, an' exactly how much you had, right down t'the last nickle. An' uh – just how much did you have, little brother?'

Critch shot him a furious look; again almost maddened to the point of physical violence. Then, getting control of himself, he decided that Arlie quite likely *didn't* know the amount of the theft. He didn't, since it would have been highly impractical for him to have stolen the money himself. Instead, he had had that Indian youth steal it – I.K., or whatever his name was – arranging to meet with him later for a division of the money. (A division which would profit the Indian damned little.)

'Yeah, little brother? How much did you say you had?'

Critch hesitated, a vengeful idea coming into his mind. Suppose he told Arlie that the sum was much larger than it was. Arlie would naturally demand that the Indian produce that amount, and when he couldn't – well, all hell would pop, right? That Apache kid was obviously capable of a great deal of nastiness – as, needless to say, was Arlie. And if the two of them should get in a fight—

Huh-uh; Critch mentally shook his head to the notion. Revenge he could do without, at least for the present. His pre-eminent need was the money, and his best chance of getting it back was to have Arlie get it. A friendly Arlie – one who believed that little

102

brother, Critch, was friendly toward him and entirely unsuspecting of his duplicity.

So, now, Critch raised somber eyes to his brother's face; heaved a huge sigh as Arlie prompted him yet a third time.

'Arlie,' he said. 'I'll tell you, but I want you to keep it in strict confidence. I can trust you to do that, can't I?'

'You know you can, boy,' Arlie declared warmly. 'Just you ask, an' that's the way it'll be.'

'I'd rather you didn't even tell Paw. He'd probably get all upset, like old people do sometimes, so why worry him about it?'

'Why, sure, sure. No point to it at all. So, how much . . . ?'

'Seventy-two thousand dollars.'

'Seventy-two thousand dollars,' Arlie nodded. 'Well, now—'

He broke off with a gasp, lurched out of his tilted-back chair. He stared at Critch, mouth working wordlessly. Shakily pointing a finger at him as he tried to find his voice.

'Y-You said . . . You said – *Naw*! No, by God!'

'Yes, Arlie. Yes.'

'Holy howling owls! Where did you get—' He broke off, again; stared at Critch in open admiration. 'Critch, boy, I got to hand it to you! Gettin' yourself a whole seventy-two thousand dollars and without gettin' yourself wanted. That's right, ain't it?' he added, a trifle anxiously. 'You ain't wanted? Ain't no one comin' after you for that money?'

Critch shook his head. 'No one,' he said. 'I'm in the clear.'

'No one at all?' Arlie insisted. 'You're sure of it?'

'Positive. I wish I was even a tenth as sure of getting the money back.'

Arlie mumbled commiseratingly. He said that maybe he ought to be sort of looking around for the lousy, lowdown thief. Might just get lucky and run into him.

'Meantime,' he said, putting on his hat. 'Don't you worry none about havin' a stake to go home on. I'll see t'that, and you can count on it!'

'Yes?'

'You know. You know how danged funny Paw is. Show up there without a nice little stake, two-three thousand dollars, anyways, he'd figure you was a bum. So, by gollies, I'll get you the money, little brother! I know my way around this town, an' I got plenty of friends here. So I'll get it, one way or another.'

Critch murmured his thanks; said he would never forget the favor. His situation suddenly looked brighter to him. Several thousand dollars spent in the right places would practically guarantee his recovering the money. It would take time, of course. He would have to do some traveling, make certain arrangements with certain people; so, naturally, he could not return to the Junction with Arlie. But that was all right. He'd leave a note for the latter, regretfully explaining that he had doubted his ability to adjust to ranch life after so long an absence, and was thus going his own way, gladly forfeiting any claims to an inheritance in favor of his beloved brother. Old Ike would be disappointed, and Arlie might be suspicious for a time. But—

'. . . be on my way, Critch, boy,' Arlie was saying, as he started toward the door. 'Now, how about somethin' t' eat, huh? Want me to send you up some supper from the dinin' room?'

'Fine, fine!' Critch smiled. 'Have to get myself straightened out if I'm seeing Paw tomorrow.'

'No ifs about it,' Arlie declared. 'Said I'd get you a nice stake t'go home on, an' I'm gonna do it. So you just eat an' get yourself a good night's sleep, an' I'll see you in the morning.'

'*Morning?*' Critch said. 'B-but – but—'

'Yeah?' Arlie looked at him curiously. 'What's the matter, little brother? No need t'be botherin' you before morning, is there?'

'No *need* to! But – but what about the money you were getting for me?'

'What about it? You got plenty for anything you need tonight. Soon as we're on the train in the mornin' I'll give you the other; enough to put you on the good side of Paw.'

'B-But—'

'But what? You sure wouldn't want a lot of money on you overnight, would you?' Arlie frowned. 'That wouldn't make no sense at all, it seems to me. You get yourself robbed again after me gettin' you up a new stake, you'd really be out of luck.'

Critch stared at him helplessly, trying to frame some plausible protest; some reasonable objection to his brother's reasoning. There was, of course, none to find. He had been out-thought just as he been out-fought. And fraud having failed him, he had nothing to lose by frankness.

'Arlie,' he said quietly, 'why do you want me to come back to the Junction?'

'Why?' Arlie said. 'Well, now, why wouldn't I want you to? After all, we're brothers—'

'We're also Kings. *King* brothers, Arlie.'

'Well,' Arlie hesitated. 'I reckon we are a little different from other folks. But—'

'We're different all right. It was bred into us. Paw was more savage than civilized. Between him and Tepaha we were raised to believe that it was all right to do almost anything as long as you got away with it. As for our mother . . . well, she wound up selling her ass to all comers. Selling it or giving it away; she really didn't seem to care which.'

Arlie let out a guffaw. 'No kiddin'? Well, she was built for it, as I recall. All ass and no brains? Why, I remember one time when – uh – Well, never mind,' he concluded uncomfortably. 'Reckon it ain't really right t'be dirty-talkin' our own Maw.'

'But it's appropriate for a King. Right and wrong don't enter into the picture. So I'll ask you again, Arlie. Why do you want me at the Junction?'

Arlie said he just did, that was why. What was so God damned strange about wanting your own brother with you?

'Maybe we got kind of twisted as kids. Maybe we done plenty of wrong things in our lives. But we can change, can't we? Nothin' that says we got to keep on goin' the way we started out.'

'Forget it,' Critch said. 'Forget that I asked you.'

'But – well, dammit, I need you, boy! The ranch is just too big a job to handle by myself.'

'And I'll be a great help, won't I?' Critch shook his head cynically. 'A city dude – a man who hasn't even sat on a horse in years. Any twenty-a-month cowhand would be ten times as helpful as I would.'

'But he wouldn't be a King! Just wouldn't be fittin' to have no one else but a King runnin' things.'

'Whatever you say, Arlie,' Critch shrugged. 'Whatever you say.'

He yawned elaborately, stretched out on the bed with his hands under his head. He closed his eyes, with a murmur of apology; opening them for a moment with apparent surprise at finding Arlie still present.

'Something else?' he said.

'You're God damned right there's something else! I tell a fella somethin', I don't want him callin' me a liar!'

'Oh, I don't blame you,' Critch said earnestly. 'I've never liked it either. Of course, there is a way of avoiding it . . .'

He allowed his voice to trail off into silence, giving his brother a look of preternatural solemnity. Arlie scowled furiously, started to say something, then turned to the door and yanked it open. On the point of slamming it, he turned again and faced his brother. Grinning good-naturedly; his expression more or less back to normal.

'All right, little brother. All right. I just might have another reason for wantin' you back at the Junction.'

'You just might,' Critch agreed.

''Course, I ain't sayin' that that *is* the reason. But it might be I'd feel a lot safer that way. Might figure it'd be a lot easier to look out for you, if I knew exactly where to look out.'

'There's another side to that coin, of course.'

'Meanin', the more distance there was between us the safer I'd be?' Arlie shook his head, grinning. 'Huh-uh, little brother. Huh-uh. Because I know something about you that you don't even know yourself.'

'Such as?'

'Such as somethin' you can't do. Oh, you think you can. Prob'ly thought about doin' it plenty of times. Prob'ly even *planned* t'do it. But it's God danged lucky you never tried, because you couldn't no more do it than you could rub your ass an' your elbow at the same time. An' the reason I know you can't do it is because I *can* an' I know what it takes. An' you ain't got what it takes, little brother. You just ain't got it.'

'I ain't got what it takes,' said Critch, 'to do what?'

'To kill. You could maybe hire it done. I figure you maybe *might* hire it done if you was in the proper fix t'do it. So . . .' Arlie's drawl faded off into the silence, his grin dying with it. And once again he became the concerned big brother, the doer of good deeds. 'So,' he resumed slowly. 'So I reckon it's a plumb fine idea for you to come back to the Junction with me, Critch. Don't you? Don't you reckon it's just about the finest idea a fella ever had?'

Critch nodded dully. 'Plumb fine,' he said.

INTERLUDE

Arlie went to I.K.'s sleazy hotel around midnight. The Indian youth had a half-breed whore with him, but he had remained dressed in anticipation of young King's visit; and he promptly handed over a sheaf of thousand-dollar bills as soon as he had dismissed the naked girl. Arlie counted the money; emitted an awed whistle of appreciation. 'God damn! A whole ten thousand dollars, huh?'

'I steal good, yes?' I.K. beamed modestly. 'Do plenty all right for my ol' frien', Arlie?'

'Uh-hah, plenty,' Arlie drawled. 'Kinda puzzlin', though. I coulda sworn that Critch had maybe a dozen packets of dough stashed in that coat of his instead of just one.'

'Did have,' I.K. nodded promptly. 'I get bank to cash into t'ousand-dollar bills. Make easier to carry, you know.'

Arlie said that that had been real smart of him. And kinda dumb of the bank, when you come to think of it. 'They didn't ask you no questions, huh? Didn't want to know how come a God damned greasy-assed Injun kid like you got himself so much money?'

I.K. made a sudden dive for the door. Arlie caught him, and twisted an arm behind his back. Not until the Apache youth was on the verge of having his shoulder dislocated, did he at last gasp out a confession. 'Up there! Behin' chimney hole!'

109

Arlie pried loose the flowered-tin cover of the chimney outlet, and scooped the money out onto the bed. Counting it methodically he discovered the amount to be a hundred dollars short of seventy-two thousand. I.K. sulkily explained the shortage. 'Cash bill with dirty t'ief bartender. Give me thirty dollars for hundred.'

'Thirty dollars, huh?' Arlie said, taking out his wallet. 'Well, here's thirty more for you. You be real careful with your spendin', an' you can live on it for quite a while.'

I.K. cursed him vilely. 'God damn you, ol' Arlie! You promise me half!'

Arlie said, well, that made them both pretty sneaky, didn't it? Anyway, he continued, it would do the youth no good if he was given all the money. It would go into the pockets of smarter thieves, and he would go into jail in less than a week.

I.K. cursed him at length. He pleaded. Abruptly, he attempted an attack. The cursing and begging accomplished nothing, of course. Anticipating the attack, Arlie fended it off with a suddenly outthrust boot, the spur of which ripped the Apache's pantsleg from top to bottom.

Arlie whooped with laughter at sight of the ruined trousers. I.K. continued to scowl and curse for a time, then joined in the laughter. Arlie took a pint bottle from his hip pocket, and they drank together. Friends, to all appearances.

To all appearances . . .

For it was not the Apache way – it was not I.K.'s way – to betray one's intentions with a display of enmity.

CHAPTER ONE

a

In her room at the King's Junction ranchhouse-hotel – the room which she had formerly shared with her late husband, Boz – Joshie King drew the window shade tight, stealthily lit the coal-oil lamp and stood facing the mirror. Naked, she shivered a little with the early morning chill; shivered also with the tantalizing, demanding urge which had seethed through her plump little body since the day, three weeks before, when she had seen Critch for the first time. *God damn, she thought,* thinking the words with the complete innocence with which she would have spoken them, without reference to their meaning. *God damn, he pound my stuff plenty soon, I betcha! That Critch, he screw me good!*

Placing her hands behind her head, she examined her armpits – entirely hairless now, painfully denuded a hair at a time. She had seen pictures of bare-shouldered women, women in evening gowns; deciding, after the closest scrunity, that they had no hair in the pits of their arms. She was not sure whether they were born that way, or whether they had achieved the condition themselves. But she was sure that such swell-lookin' women, with all their little niceties, were the kind that would appeal to a swell-lookin' fella like Critch. And she was prepared to go to any lengths to make herself like them.

She sat down on the edge of the bed, and looked thoughtfully down at herself. Despite her tightly plaited hair, with its comcomitant tightening of her facial tissues, her brow puckered in a puzzled frown.

Well, she thought, were they or weren't they? Were those swell-lookin' women only hairless between their arms, or was the area surrounding their stuff also without hair?

There was no way of knowing, she guessed. Despite her most earnest searching, she had been unable to find a picture of a woman – swell-lookin' or otherwise – in the nude.

Joshie scowled, pondering the riddle. Then, hesitantly, her hand went to her crotch, and she began a half-hearted plucking of its tightly curled hair. She ceased almost as soon as she began. It hurt too God damned much, and it also impinged upon a practice which was strictly tabu.

At any rate, what did it matter, what did it really matter whether she was haired or hairless there? Critch had been pleasant to her since his return to the Junction three weeks before, but he had carefully avoided anything resembling an overture either on his part or hers.

That he wanted her, she was sure. Wanted her as badly as she wanted him. But he definitely did not want, and was determined not to have, the inevitable result of an intimate relationship.

Critch would have great plans for the future. A swell-lookin' fella like Critch would *have* to have. And there would be no room in such plans for an Apache bride.

He would have no squaw for a wife, not Critch King. He wouldn't, because he had no intention of staying here on the ranch a day longer than he had to.

Joshie was sure of it. Everyone else apparently thought otherwise, including Old Uncle Ike and Old Grandfather Tepaha. But Joshie knew better. She had had more opportunity than anyone else to observe Critch, to study his attitude and read between the lines of his speech. And she *knew*.

Bleakly, she turned despairing eyes upon the mirror, looking into it and beyond to a future of loveless emptiness.

There could be no man for her but a King. This was so, a fact accepted by all. Something that could not be changed, and which she could not contemplate changing.

She would have Critch or no one. And she could not possibly have Critch. Unless . . .

What if his life depended upon her?

What if she had certain information which could compel him to marry her?

She glanced toward the window; noted, in the thin margin between casing and shade, a grayish adulteration of the darkness which presaged dawn. Arlie and her sister, Kay, Arlie's wife, should be awake by now. Awake and talking. That much Joshie knew from her past eavesdropping outside their door. And while she had learned virtually nothing that was of use to her, nothing that she could piece together into the complete and conclusive, she had heard enough to be tantalized. For one thing – one very important thing – she had become reasonably certain that Kay was suspicious of Critch's intentions toward Arlie. And Kay's suspicions, Joshie knew, were not likely to remain merely that. Sooner or later – very, very soon, in all likelihood – Kay would see to it that they were translated into action.

It had been so with Boz.

It would be so with Critch.

And, by God, she God damn well better not! Joshie thought hotly. Critch gonna be my ol' husband!

Still, and despite what she herself was sure of, Joshie had no concrete proof. Most of what she knew was merely instinctive, knowledge born of knowledge of her sister rather than what her sister had said. Kay had said nothing which could be pointed to as evidence, and Arlie had said even less. And until they did say something utterly damning and incriminating, and impossible to explain away . . .

Joshie stood up. She pulled a short cotton shift over her head, a garment made of flour sacks. Silently, she left the room, crossed the hall to the door of her sister and brother-in-law. She sank to her knees, then lay flat on her stomach on the carpet runner, her ear pressed tightly against the aperture at the base of the door.

A strong draft swept through it: their window was open, and a morning breeze was sweeping across the room, sweeping the room's sounds before it to the tensely listening Joshie.

She could hear everything as clearly as though she were in the room with Kay and Arlie. But all she could hear for a time was the measured creaking of the bed, and the quickening tumult of copulation to climax.

Then, after a period of contented quiet . . .

b

Arlie withdrew from his wife's full body; flopped down on his back at her side. 'Now, by God,' he declared, 'that's what I call a prime piece of meat! The more I get, the better it gets.'

114

Kay giggled, pleasedly, then suddenly made herself silent and drew slightly away from him. Arlie asked what the hell was the matter with her. Kay said there was no point in telling him. After all, she was only his wife, and a person of no consequence. Arlie let out a groan.

'Now, God damn it, ol' squaw—!'

'See? What I tell you?' Kay demanded. 'I tell you somet'ing for your own good, an'—'

'Well, I ain't gonna tell you nothing for your own good,' Arlie asserted. 'I'm gonna *do* something! Just one more God damned word out of you about Critch, an' I'm—'

'Hokay, hokay,' Kay shrugged. 'I *not* say one more God damn word. But by God, maybe some day you wish I had, I betcha.'

Arlie said, 'Oh, shit!' very loudly. There was a considerable silence after this, as Kay assumed an attitude of haughty hurt. At last, Arlie gave one of her breasts an affectionate pinch, and asked her why such a pretty little squaw had to be such a big horse's ass.

'I'm tellin' you, honey. I've said it before an' I'll say it again. Ol' Critch, he couldn't kill a baby chigger if it was chewin' his dong off.'

'Ho!' sniffed Kay. 'So you say, an I say how come? He a King, ain't he? You kill, Ol' Boz kill, Ol' Uncle Ike kill. All Kings plenty mean sonsabitches. All killers. So how come not Critch?'

Arlie wet his lips hesitantly. 'I don't know why,' he admitted. 'But I still know it. Maybe he got away from here young enough, so's he growed up different. Anyways, it just ain't in him t'kill no one.'

'Then, how he get all that money? You t'ink maybe some one jus' give it to him?'

'God damn it, don't you listen to nothin' I say? I told you Critch wasn't a killer. Which don't mean that he ain't the smoothest, sneakiest, crookedest son-of-a-bitch that ever come down the pike.'

'So he crooks somebody for money. Beeg, beeg money like U.S. treasury department, an Ol' Critch he get it. Fool people plenty.'

'That's for sure, Ol' squaw.'

'Critch plenty good foolin' people. Maybe so he fool you.'

'Oh, for shit's sake—!' Arlie slapped his forehead. 'I'll tell you who he fooled! Some God damn stupid woman like you!'

The outburst was purely retaliatory, its substance mere irritation. Not until the words were out of his mouth, did he consider their portent; that what he had said in thoughtless anger was quite likely true.

By God, it made sense, didn't it? Lacking the guts to kill, Critch would logically choose women to victimize. He had screwed some woman for the seventy-two thousand; doubtless screwed her literally as well as figuratively.

What woman would be carrying so much cash? Why hadn't she appealed to the law, thus making Critch a wanted man – which he definitely was not?

The answer came to Arlie almost simultaneously with the question. The woman hadn't kicked because she couldn't. She was wanted herself. And . . .

Those Anderson sisters! Critch had almost stared a hole in the wanted posters on them. Looked at 'em so long that Marshal Thompson had been half-way suspicious. And ol' Critch had covered up pretty well, being such a smooth, sneaky bastard. But still—

Had Critch swindled both of the sisters or only

one? How had he, no killer, managed to rob a woman (or women) who killed for a living?

'. . . well. *Well?*' Kay's voice cut in on his thoughts. 'You answer me, ol' Arlie!'

Arlie yawned elaborately, mumbled that he must have dozed off for a minute. 'What the hell you jabberin' about now?'

'I say,' repeated Kay firmly, 'that everyone kill sometime, 'bout something, even ol' Critch. Right now, he t'ink maybe he get money back, so he don't do nothin'. But he find out money gone, *zzzzt*, you be dead, ol' husband.'

Arlie groaned. Silently cursed himself for telling her about the money, and deciding to be very cautious in confiding in her henceforth.

'Ol' Uncle Ike, he like Critch better'n you. Maybe so some day Critch own ranch, an' you be up shit creek.'

Arlie grunted that she had obviously been up the creek herself and swallowed too much of its contents. 'Critch is just someone new for Paw to talk to, an' he ain't seen Critch since he was a kid. Soon as the newness wears off, he'll be just as rough on Critch as he is on everyone.'

'Ho,' said Kay.

'Ho, ho!' said Arlie.

'Ol' Uncle Ike, he buys skinny cigars Critch like. He buy special extra fine whiskey Critch like. An' all the time, he make talk with Critch. Ol' Uncle Ike, he say, Arlie, go do this, do that; I will talk with Critch.'

'But God damn it, I just got through telling you—! I mean, uh, if you didn't keep your jaw goin' all the time like the clatter-bone in a duck's ass, an' I ever got a chance to think—!'

117

Kay turned on her side, pulled his head against her breast and gave him a motherly caress. She kissed him gently, softly stroking his hair; holding him protectively close. Of course, he should think, she said; and whatever he thought would be right, because he was her ol' Arlie an' he always knew what was best.

Arlie sighed, a mixture of contentment and protest. 'I thought you'd changed your mind about Critch. Thought you had him tabbed for Joshie's man.'

'Did,' admitted Kay. 'But that before I see danger. Mus' take care of husband first. Ol' Joshie, she do same thing with Critch. Ol' Boz no God damn good or she take care of him, too.'

Arlie hesitated.

'Well,' he said. 'I guess there's no hell of a big hurry about Critch. Nothin' I got to rush into.'

'You no think so, Arlie? My ver', ver' smart ol' husband he really think there no hurry?'

There was an insidiously incredulous note to her voice; a note of stunned astonishment. Thus, a mother might address an adult son who has just wet his Sunday britches.

'Well, but, looky,' Arlie squirmed. 'Marshal Thompson already put me on warning, an' he damn well meant what he said. I go for Critch, Marshal Thompson' gonna be comin' for me!'

'Maybe so Critch have accident,' Kay suggested smoothly. 'Critch have accident not your fault.'

'Well,' Arlie said. 'Well . . .'

'My ol' Arlie, he plenty sneaky devil,' Kay said flatteringly. 'He fix up plenty bad accident on ol' Critch, an' nobody prove it not accident. I know, by God!'

She kissed him again. Resumed her hypnotic stroking of his head. But Arlie was not yet won over. Or if he was, he did not say so.

He flung back the covers suddenly, and swung his feet to the floor.

'Time to get up,' he announced. 'Pile out, ol' squaw.'

He stood up, began pulling on his clothes.

Outside the door, Joshie also stood up and silently returned to her room.

c

In his room, Critch King also began dressing; now and then wincing or stifling a groan as his movements twisted some saddle-tortured-muscle or joint. His first week had been pure murder for him. Every day he had silently sworn that he could not take another day. Every morning it had been a monumental struggle to get out of bed, and he had had to fight to keep from begging off for the day. He had mustered up the strength and courage to resist such an admission of weakness only because he had to. For despite the surprising amiability – even favoritism – which his father had shown toward him, he well knew Old Ike's detestation of weakness. Ike simply would not tolerate it in a son, any more than he would have tolerated improvidence. And since Critch had to remain at the Junction, at least until he recovered his stolen money, and he could only remain there by living up to the old man's standards – well, somehow he had done it. He had never thought he could, but he had. And now, after three weeks, what had once seemed unbearable was now merely difficult, and less and less difficult with each passing day.

In the flickering light of the kerosene lamp, he studied himself in the dresser mirror; felt a kind of abashed pride at the change in his appearance. The normal olive pallor of his face had given way to heavy tan. He had gained weight; even his shoulders appeared to have broadened. His clothes, garments virtually identical with those worn by Tepaha, Arlie and Ike, now fitted him snugly whereas they had originally seemed to hang on him.

He glanced down at his hands, grinned sourly at their appearance. They were calloused, stiff, the nails torn and stubby. But, never mind. Money and time would take care of such trifles. He would have the first and hence the last as soon as he had evened the score with Arlie. For the time being, he must move slowly. Giving Arlie time to become unwary and let his guard down; working to ingratiate himself even further with Old Ike; getting into the good graces of everyone who might later prove useful to him.

All he had to do was what he had been doing. Work – and wait for opportunity to reveal itself. And for seventy-two thousand dollars he was prepared to work and wait indefinitely.

Critch finished dressing, putting the final touch to his costume by tucking a knife into his boot-top. The knife was expected of him, and he was doing what was expected. Also, he had been practising with it at night. Shadow-fighting before the mirror until he was too exhausted to make another feint.

It could come in very handy some day. He just might give Brother Arlie the surprise of a lifetime.

Taking a final look at himself, Critch lounged near the door, waiting for the sound of the others emerging from their rooms. Meanwhile, speculating on just where Arlie had hidden the money.

He was confident that Arlie had not left it in El Reno, but had brought it back to the ranch with him. For once, on the return trip to the Junction, Arlie had left him alone in their stateroom for a few moments, and Critch had seized the opportunity to search his brother's carpetbag. And buried at the bottom of it, beneath several articles of clothing, was a heavy steel box.

It was a brand-new box, with the El Reno merchant's price tag still on it. Shaking it, Critch had heard a telltale rustling, a softish series of thuds from within. He was debating what to do – whether to take the box and risk leaping from the window – when he heard Arlie at the door. So he had hastily jammed the receptacle back where he had gotten it, and reclosed the carpetbag. And that had been his last chance to recover the money.

For the rest of their ride, Arlie had ridden with his feet on the bag, or taken it with him whenever he left the stateroom.

Now, Critch heard familiar sounds in the hallway, and he stepped out into it. He said good-morning to Arlie, nodded at Kay and gave a warm smile to Joshie. Then, the four of them started down the stairs, Arlie and Critch in front, Kay walking behind her husband and Joshie behind Critch.

They were nearing the foot of the staircase when there was a scurrying scuffle, an angrily sibilant whispering from the two girls. Arlie whirled around, gave each a long slow look. But their round dolls' faces with the preternaturally widened eyes were prim masks of innocence. So the descent continued, and the foursome continued on into the bar where Tepaha and Ike awaited them.

Drinks were poured for the men, Critch's from a

special bottle which Arlie stared at meaningfully. They toasted each other silently, tossed down the liquor at a gulp; thudded their glasses back to the table. Old Ike hoisted himself up from his chair, turned to lead the way into the dining room. And Kay suddenly let out a yell.

'*Ouch!* God damn, plenty ouch, by God!'

Simultaneously, she began to hop about on one moccasined foot, clutching the other in her hands.

Tepaha leaped forward. Grabbing her shoulders, he gave her a vigorous shake; demanded the reason for her outrageous breach of decorum.

'Speak, witless girl! Stop dancing like crazy chicken and explain, or I slap you loose from pants!'

Kay gingerly lowered her foot to the floor, looked murderously at her sister.

'Ol' Joshie stamp on my foot, Grandfather. Hurt like hell.'

'So!' said Tepaha, turning ominously to Joshie. 'Did you stamp on your sister's foot? *Did you?*'

Joshie nodded nervously, sullenly, adding that Kay had invited the attack.

'Ol' Kay say mean things, Grandfather Tepaha. I try to make her stop, but she keep on.'

'That is no excuse,' Tepaha declared sternly. 'One wrong does not right another.' He hesitated, one hand drawn back. 'What were these mean things?'

'Well—' Joshie fidgeted, her eyes downcast. 'She say – she say—'

'Speak quickly, foolish child!'

'S-She say . . . she—' Joshie's voice suddenly strengthened, blurting out the words. 'She say I want ol' Critch to fock my possy! She say my possy no good, so he no fock me!'

Tepaha blinked, let out a stunned grunt. He

looked at Ike, a look that silently appealed for help. But his old friend had averted his eyes, and was convulsed by a spasm of coughing.

Helplessly, Tepaha shifted his gaze back to Joshie. 'Such words are spoken only between man and woman,' he said. 'Privately. You will have to be punished.'

His arm arced for a slap. Critch spoke up quickly.

'Pardon me, Grandfather, but Kay spoke the words first. Joshie only repeated them at your request.'

'Well—' Tepaha hesitated; nodded. 'You speak truth, Critch. Stand forward, Kay.'

'Now, just a God damn minute!' Arlie snapped. 'What about Joshie stomping on Kay's foot? What about that, huh? And' – glaring at Critch. 'Just where the hell you get off buttin' into this? You got nothin' to say about Kay or Joshie neither! She ain't your squaw.'

'Now, Arlie,' Critch said mildly. 'After all, fair is fair—'

'Fair is shit! If Kay gets slapped, then by God Joshie gets it! It's both of 'em or neither!'

Tepaha's face hardened. Arlie put a protective arm around Kay, and Joshie moved closer to Critch. Silence fell over the room as one stubborn glare locked with another. Then, old Ike found his voice, declared firmly that the matter was to be dropped.

'Not another God damn word out o' no one, or by God I'll do a hell of a lot more than slap! Now, they's work to be done an' breakfast t'be et before, so let's get at it.'

He led the way into the dining room.

Tepaha stalked behind him, after a stern glare at the four young people.

Arlie followed, followed by his wife. Critch, trailed by Joshie, entered last. As, of course, was proper for the youngest son.

The meal was a huge one, consisting mainly of meat: steak, pork chops and ribs, slices of venison roast. Along with the meat, there were eggs, cracked-corn porridge, stewed dried fruit, biscuits, cornbread and buckwheat cakes. There was milk also – canned milk. As on many ranches, even today, all effort was concentrated on the production of beef. A cow's milk went to suckle her calf, without a drop's diversion to human beings.

The meal was cooked, and also served, by squaws; kinswomen, by blood or marriage, to the workmen in the Junction's several business establishments: the blacksmith shop, the feed and grain store, and the general store.

There was virtually no talk at the table, everyone emulating Ike and Tepaha in disposing of as much food as possible in the time allotted for breakfast. Critch had failed to do this, in the beginning; fastidiously picking at his food, and feeling a little ill at the gorging of the others. The result was that he had almost collapsed from weakness in midmorning. And by the time the sun was directly overhead, signalling the lunch hour, he had toppled rather than climbed down from his saddle.

At last, Old Ike glanced at his turnip-like watch, belched heavily, and shoved back his plate. Tepaha also belched and leaned back from the table. In short, the meal was over.

Ike caught Arlie's eye, and nodded to him. 'You an' Kay go saddle up. You're gettin' a late start this mornin'.'

'Me an' Kay again, huh?' Arlie scowled. 'How

come it ain't never Critch and Joshie.'

Ike ignored him, turning to Joshie. 'Go bring Critch's bottle, an' some of his seegars. We got talk to make.'

Joshie said, 'Yes, Old Uncle,' and scurried away, giving her sister a triumphant sneer. Still ignoring Arlie, Ike spoke to Critch: How did Critch feel about ranch work by now? Was everyone treatin' him all right? Was there anything he needed? Critch murmured appropriate replies, nervously aware of his brother's displeasure. Arlie flung back his chair suddenly. He stamped out of the room, moving so fast that Kay was forced to run to keep up with him.

'So everything's goin' all right?' Ike asked, as Joshie poured after-breakfast drinks. 'Any questions about the work or anythin'?'

'None so far,' Critch smiled. 'None, that is, that Arlie hasn't been able to answer.'

'They's maybe plenty Arlie can learn from you. You figure he needs to know somethin', you speak up.'

Critch nodded, without the slightest intention of carrying out his father's order. Arlie's hurt pride and huffiness must not be turned into anger. Moreover, he could hardly suggest improvements in a routine, which, while arduous, was the essence of simplicity.

The day's work consisted of merely visiting the holdings of one Apache tenant after another. At each place, Arlie and Critch consulted with the head of the family, inquiring into his progress, taking note of his needs and offering such advice as seemed indicated. Meanwhile, Joshie and Kay performed much the same chore for the household's womenfolk.

'Lessee, now,' Old Ike rumbled. 'The four of you is still ridin' together, right? Maybe you ought to be splittin' up into twos, so's you could cover more ground.'

'Well . . .' Critch hesitated. 'If you think I'm ready . . .'

Ike said it wasn't what *he* thought, but what Critch thought that mattered. 'Make up your own mind,' he added, hoisting his heavy body from his chair. 'Now, you better be skedaddlin' out o' here.'

d

Old Ike and Old Tepaha retired to the bar room for a time, each napping briefly, head on chest, though both would have denied it. They awakened simultaneously, and went for a highly critical tour of the Junction's commercial facilities. It was nearing train time by then, so they walked down to the depot. The agent-telegrapher, a half-breed who lived primitively on the premises, treated them to coffee and amiable insults. In the distance, the train hooted its approach and they went outside to greet it.

It came and went, leaving not an iota of mail. Not a single dun or notice of creditor's judgement. It had been so for many days now, more days than Old Ike's memory – a memory that was responsive only to things in the distant past rather than the immediate – could accurately recall.

With relief and puzzlement, he pondered the riddle aloud.

Tepaha declared that the answer was simple. 'All bad men. Bad men make bad enemies. Maybe so all get killed, I betcha.'

'All 't once? That don't make sense.'

'Huh! What makes sense, then, you so God damn smart?'

126

'Well . . . I reckon they just figured I was an A-1 honest fella that wasn't out to beat no one for his money – like they'd've knowed in the first place if they had any God damn sense – so they ups and decides t'stop pesterin' me.'

'Ho! You one crazy shit, ol' Ike.'

'What's crazy about it, you dried up ol' son-of-a-bitch?'

'Huh! I say maybe all get killed, all 't once, you say don't make sense. You say all get nice-nice all 't once, I say you don't make no sense. Same God damn thing, by God, only I smarter'n you. Enemies like fleas on dead dog. No nice-nice never. Bite him till he dies.'

Arguing crotchetily, the two old men walked back toward the hotel. And at last Ike yawned, losing interest in the discussion. Ending it with the statement that he was content with the fact that his creditors were leaving him alone, and he didn't care a cow turd why they were doing it.

'Now' – he suppressed another yawn, turning into the hotel's bar, 'we'll just have ourselves a little drink, an' then I'm goin' up to my room. Got some plannin' I got to do.'

'I also have plans to make,' Tepaha declared with great dignity, 'and must do so in my room.'

They drank.

They went up the stairs together. Each leaning slightly against the other, each supporting the other with his body.

At the head of the stairs, they stood panting for a time. Then, as they trudged slowly down the hall toward their rooms and beds, Tepaha addressed his friend. Speaking in Spanish as do all wise men when treating of delicate and painful matters.

127

'Great evil may derive from one pure in heart. He is blind to the mottled snake in the corn rows.'

'And kindness can be as a dagger,' Ike nodded. 'Tell me thou, what is in thy heart?'

'So. Then I tell you that you are creating bad blood between your sons. In clutching Critch too closely to your bosom, you are thrusting Arlie aside.'

'This . . . this I know.' Old Ike bowed his head. 'It is something I cannot help.'

'Cannot? Cannot becomes unbelievable on the lips of Old Ike King.' Tepaha hesitated. 'Is it because of her? You see her image in Critch?'

'Perhaps. But I see much more than that. I see a small boy thrust away from me when I should have held him closely to my heart. The time I have to spend with him does not equal the years that I spent without him.'

'But, Ike, my dear friend—'

'No. I cannot change what I was, friend Tepaha, and I cannot change what I am. Nor what I do. The heart is its own master, O, Tepaha, and you have entered a room where only I can dwell. Leave now, and do not return.'

'It shall be as you say,' Tepaha said.

Spanish was abandoned at this point, and they slid back into their everyday vernacular. Old Ike grunted that he would see Tepaha in an hour or so, as soon as he finished his planning, which was extensive and arduous since he had to do it for everyone.

'These God damn kids, nowadays, Tepaha; they ain't like we was. Have to tell 'em when to piss or it'd be runnin' out their ears.'

'Arlie plenty smart boy,' Tepaha said. 'Work damn hard, too.'

'Yeah, hell,' Old Ike said. 'I guess so. Who the hell said he wasn't?'

''Course, Critch plenty damn smart, too . . .'

'You're God damn right he is! Brought more'n three thousand dollars home with him, an' he was all dressed up an' talkin' as fine as the president of the U.S. An' – an'—'

'Also, he be good worker, come by an' by. Maybe so as good as Arlie.'

'What d'ya mean, maybe so, come by an' by?' Ike bellowed. 'He's as good now, you stupid old shit!'

He yanked open the door to his room, entered it and slammed the door behind him. Sitting down heavily on the bed, he toed his boots off and sank back on the pillows with a grateful sigh.

He had not meant to be like this . . .

Stubbornly, he had set up certain barriers between himself and his errant son; grimly leaving it to Critch to surmount those barriers or to remain away forever.

And Critch had surmounted them. Climbed over them unscathed, and returned home in grandeur. A young man handsome as sin, and smart as paint. And—

An' hell. Hell, wasn't he entitled to a little favorin'? A little somethin' extra? Why, hell, he was kinda like a visitor, a guest, an' a fella that didn't put himself out a mite for a guest was a pretty sorry son-of-a-bitch. An' when someone was more'n a visitor, your youngest son that you hadn't seen in years, what the hell was wrong with makin' sure that he knew he was welcome?

. . . The heart is its own master, and Ike dwelt in a chamber where there was room for no other.

And he slept.

CHAPTER TWO

a

Now, in this first hour after dawn, the village of King's Junction was wide awake and working. A hammer rang on the anvil of the blacksmith's shop. At the feed store a wagon was being loaded. Apache clerks, apron bedecked over their buckskin and levi costumes, were washing windows and sweeping the wooden walk of the general store.

As the two King brothers rode out of town, Tepaha's two grand-daughters riding behind them, Arlie was greeted by and gave greeting to the Junction's various workers. But he had not a word nor a glance for Critch. Similarly, Joshie and Kay rode in haughty silence, neither acknowledging the other's presence with so much as a look.

Critch lighted a cheroot, made a tentative gesture of offering one to Arlie. The latter looked stonily straight ahead, and Critch returned the cigar to his pocket.

He knew the reason for Arlie's attitude, or thought he did: Old Ike's cozying up to him, his youngest son. Yet there was nothing new in this: Ike had been behaving thus ever since his return. So why should Arlie take such great offense this morning?

Had Arlie simply had too much of it? Or had something else happened that he, Critch, was unaware of?

He didn't know, but he knew that Arlie's anger could not be allowed to continue. Until he recovered the money, he must stay on his brother's good side.

They crossed the railroad tracks, and took one of the rutted, reddish-loam roads which led out into the ranch proper. Wordlessly, they rode through the fine spring morning, threadily misted with the early sun's lifting of the night's dew. Stalks of young, uneared corn wafted in the breeze like long lines of green flame. The heavy-sweet smell of embryonically budding alfalfa drifted to them from distant acres.

Critch sniffed it with exaggerated interest, hoping to attract his brother's attention. Failing to, he cleared his throat noisily.

'Uh, about that alfalfa, Arlie,' he said. 'How do you find it as a crop?'

Arlie made no answer for a time; seemingly intended to make none. Finally, however, he asked Critch what the hell he was talking about. 'What do you mean, how do I find it?'

'I mean, isn't it pretty hard on land like this? I've heard that it took a lot out of the soil, used several hundred tons of water per acre.'

'Huh. An' just where did you hear that?'

'I'm not sure,' Critch said. 'It's just something I heard or read somewhere. For all I know, it's all nonsense, but I thought you'd know the facts.'

The implied compliment was more than Arlie could resist. He said, with forced grumpiness, that, hell, how would he know what was what? He'd never been nowhere nor read nothin'.

'But I guess it ain't a real good crop for out here,' he went on, his tone warming slightly. 'Not real fittin' for the soil an' climate, an' it can be damned

131

bad for cattle. Bloats 'em to beat hell they get too much of it.'

'Yes?' Critch frowned. 'Then why is it planted?'

'Because that's what the folks that planted it wanted,' Arlie shrugged. 'It's their land, the Indians, I mean, as long as they work it. They got the say-so of what goes on it.'

'That doesn't sound like a very good way of running things,' Critch said.

'It's *their* land,' Arlie repeated. 'If a man can't do what he wants with his own, he ain't a man. That's the way the Indians look at it. That's the way Paw looks at it.'

Critch nodded, subsiding. He had broken the ice with his brother which was all he wanted to do. The Indians, for all he cared, could shove the land up their copper-skinned asses.

'I tell you something, Critch . . .' Arlie resumed, after a silence of several minutes. 'I, uh, well – I think I'll just have me one of them seegars, after all!'

Critch gave him one, smiling inwardly. Unctuously courteous, he also held a match for his brother. The thaw in their relationship seemingly had its effect on Joshie and Kay. *Seemingly*. For as the foursome jogged onward, a murmur of sporadic conversation between the sisters drifted up to the two men.

'About this morning, Arlie,' Critch began a low-voiced apology, determined to keep things on their present happy keel. 'I don't blame you for getting sore, and —'

'Oh, hell,' Arlie laughed. 'I can't blame you for Paw's doin'. Anyways, I wasn't 'specially sore about that. I just sort of got my short hairs ruffled about, well, several things. Got myself kinda nervy, you know.'

'I didn't want to come back here, Arlie. It was your idea.'

'An' it still is,' his brother said firmly. 'I just wouldn't have it no other way.'

'Well,' said Critch, 'as long as you feel— !'

'*Yeow! Damn' bitch!*' shrieked Kay.

'*Fix you, mean bitch!*' screamed Joshie.

Arlie whirled around, cursing. 'Now, what the holy hell—!' Critch also pivoted in the saddle; then, emulating his brother, he scrambled to the road and raced toward the two girls.

Each had her hands knotted in the other's braids. Each tugged with all her might as she screamed obscenities at the other. Each simultaneously released a hand and began slugging and clawing. The wild commotion caused their horses to rear and buck, pitching the two girls to the road. But the fight went on unabated. They tumbled and rolled in the dirt, hitting, scratching and gouging.

Arlie yelled for them to stop, profanely threatening punishment to come. Ignored, he tried to separate them and received a moccasined foot in his face.

'Now, by God!' – he fell back, rubbing an incipiently swelling nose. 'By Christ, that does it!'

He whipped the knife from his boot-top. Hand darting deftly, he made two delicate jabs with the needle-sharp point of the blade, sinking it a minute fraction of an inch into each girl's flaring, pear-shaped bottom.

That ended the fracas. Yipping simultaneously, they came to their feet. Began doing a little dance of pain as they gripped their bottoms. Arlie took advantage of the distraction to seize his wife and hang on to her, and Critch did likewise with Joshie.

'God damn stupid squaws!' Arlie cursed. 'What

133

the hell was that all about, huh?' And as Kay began a sulky reply, he silenced her with a shake. 'Never mind, by God! I reckon I already know. Now, just looky what you done with your crazy carryin' on.'

He pointed. All four horses had bolted during the melee, and were now scattered, grazing peacefully, about the adjacent field.

'So start movin'!' Arlie commanded. 'Get out there an' catch up them ponies. An' no more nonsense neither, or I'll make your ass smoke like a big baked potato!'

Kay backed a step or two away from him, then halted stubbornly. 'Ol' Joshie's fault, too. I go, she gotta go.'

'Now, God damn you, ol' squaw—!' Arlie took a warning stride toward her. 'You gonna move, or you want me to move you?'

Kay moved . . . a few more steps. Again halted mulishly. 'Is only fair,' she asserted. 'Joshie n' me, we both make fight. Both should go after ponies.'

'Uh-*hah!* So's you could start yourself another fight, huh?'

'No. No more fight,' Kay promised. 'But Joshie gotta go with me. Is right thing to do.'

'Well, but—' Arlie hesitated, awkwardly, cast a half pleading look at his brother. 'Critch, I don't want t'do no buttin' in on your squaw – I mean, kind of your squaw even if she ain't really – but—'

'Kay is right,' Critch agreed handsomely. 'Joshie, you go and help your sister!'

Joshie tossed her head. 'Ho, ho!' she jeered. 'Looka who's talkin'. What you say I tell you go to hell?'

'He don't say nothin'!' Arlie snapped. 'He just plops you over his knee and pounds your happy ass

134

off! I mean,' he added hastily, with a deferential glance at his brother, 'I mean, uh, that's right, ain't it, Critch? Paw an' Grandfather Tepaha don't favor beatin' up a woman, but they got nothin' against a good ass-paddlin'.'

'My own sentiments exactly,' Critch declared firmly. 'Joshie' – he pointed. 'Go and help Kay catch those ponies.'

'Huh! An' you gonna pound my ass if I don't?'

'You're damned right he is,' said Arlie. 'Right, Critch!'

'Uh, right,' Critch mumbled. 'I mean, I certainly will.'

Joshie bowed her head meekly . . . with false meekness. Inwardly titillated, warmly content with herself, she departed with her sister. They started across the field, moving ahead and to the side – each intuitively accepting her role in catching the horses – so as to come up and close in on the animals from opposite directions. The two men watched them for a few moments, Arlie opining that there was nothing like exercise for taking the orneriness out of a squaw; then, satisfied that the girls intended no more mischief, they sat down on the bank of the roadside ditch and lighted cheroots.

There was an amiable silence for several minutes. A silence at last broken by Arlie's good-natured declaration that the girls' quarreling was really Critch's fault.

'I mean it, little brother. You just bounce that Joshie around in a bed, like you ought to've done long ago, and there wouldn't be nothin' for her an' Kay t'fuss about.'

'You mean marry her?' Critch laughed irritably. 'Why, I barely know the girl.'

'You know her well enough. How the hell you gonna get to know her if you don't marry her?'

'Forget it,' Critch said. 'It's out of the question.'

'How come it is? You don't figure you're too good to marry an Indian do you? After all you're part Indian yourself.'

'On Maw's side,' Critch nodded. 'Paw's, too, for all I know – or he knows. So, naturally, it's not a question of being too good for Joshie. I'm simply not ready to marry anyone yet.'

'Well,' Arlie grumbled. 'It'd sure save a hell of a lot of trouble if you was ready. Anyways, it just ain't natural goin' on like this. You need a woman, an' Joshie needs a man.'

Critch carefully studied the tip of his cheroot; cautiously remarked that he could not disagree with his brother's belief anent the need of man for woman, and vice versa.

'I find Joshie highly desirable, and she is obviously attracted to me, so there's no problem *per se* about going to bed with her. But—'

'Sure, but you can't do it without marryin' her,' Arlie nodded. 'Naturally. An' you don't figure to marry her – not yet, anyways – so what's the use of talking about it?'

'Right,' murmured Critch. 'You're absolutely right, Arlie.' And from the corners of his eyes, he studied his brother with veiled incredulity.

For Arlie's face was guileless, utterly free of mockery. He undoubtedly had meant what he said. He could not accept the notion of extramarital sex with a grand-daughter of Tepaha.

'Lookin' kinda puzzled, Critch,' Arlie opined, giving his brother a direct look. 'Somethin' I can help you with?'

136

'What?' Critch blinked. 'Oh, no, not at all. I was just thinkin' that, uh – uh—'

'Yeah?'

'Well, uh – about us pairing off. I mean, you and Kay taking one area and Joshie and I covering another. Do you think I'm ready for that yet? Paw was saying this morning that we might give it a try – if you thought it was all right, of course.'

Arlie hesitated, chewing a stem of Johnson grass. 'Why not give it a try?' he suggested. 'Ain't really no other way of finding out whether you're up to it.'

'Right,' Critch said, adding that they'd still be ahead of the game even if the experiment proved unsuccessful. 'At least, we won't have to worry about the girls fighting for a day.'

'Now, you're talking!' Arlie declared, and he stood up, dusting the seat of his pants. 'Well, guess we're 'bout ready to ride.'

The two girls returned, each riding a horse and leading one. The four animals were portioned out to their proper owners, and the sisters were apprised of the change in plans. Then, Arlie and Kay rode off down the road together, and Critch and Joshie cut out across the field to the south.

Joshie kept her mount reined in close to Critch, ostensibly to advise him on the day's routine. As their legs brushed repeatedly, Critch attempted to pull away, but each time he was defeated. Ramblingly chattering of this and that – he could only guess at what was important – she clung close to him, pressing her thigh against his until he could feel its heat, and his nostrils were filled with the sweet smell of fecund flesh.

Unable to get away from her, he at last ceased to try. Deciding to let her have her own way, and see what she would do with it. Which, for the moment, was nothing at all. Seemingly, he had defeated her by ceasing to resist. For she suddenly became silent, her small round face creased with puzzlement. She even allowed her horse to draw away a little, relieving him of the tantalizing pressure of her body.

So they rode for a time, with Critch silently congratulating himself yet somehow disappointed by his victory. At last he risked a glance at her, and saw that she was smiling at him archly, her head flirtatiously cocked to one side. And again she brought her horse in close to his.

'I bad girl while ago,' she said, her voice softly husky with desire. 'You paddle my ass, yes?'

'W-What? No! No, of course not!' Critch snapped. 'What's the matter with you anyway?'

Joshie replied sweetly that nothing was the matter. She had been a bad squaw, and bad squaws got spanked. 'This is so,' she declared serenely. 'It is the way it has always been.'

'Well, it's not going to be that way with me!' Critch said firmly.

'How come not?' Joshie inquired. And added brightly, 'I bet you paddle ass God damn good! Pound shit right outta me!'

'Now, God damn it— !' Critch turned on her in a fury of frustration. 'What the hell is this? Are you crazy or something? Now, stop talking like that or I'm going to be very angry with you!'

Joshie gave him a look of baffled innocence. Talkin' like what? she inquired. She talked like everyone else.

'I talk plenty God damn good,' she asserted, a trace of pique coming into her voice. 'Maybe so you talk bad.'

Critch drew a deep breath, on the point of exploding. Slowly he exhaled, getting control of himself; recognizing the justice of what she said.

'I'm sorry, Joshie,' he said. 'You do talk like everyone else here, and being a minority of one, I suppose I do seem to be wrong just as you seem to be right. But—'

'Min – Min-or-ity? What is, ol' Critch?'

'A damn fool in this case,' Critch said. 'But, look, Joshie. When I was a boy, Paw hired teachers to come to the ranch. They traveled from family to family, and every child was taught to read and write. On top of that—'

'Is still same way,' the Indian girl interposed. 'Also, boy'r girl want to go 'way to school, Old Uncle Ike he send 'em.'

'Then, you did have some schooling. At least you learned simple arithmetic and how to read and write.'

Joshie said sure she had. Same as all papooses. She had not chosen to go away to school, since rarely did anyone else so choose and she had not wished to go alone. 'Too God damn lonesome,' she pointed out cheerfully. 'I be, uh – how you say – min-or-ty.'

'Minority. But what I'm getting at is this. You've had enough education to know that nice girls don't talk like you do—'

'I nice girl!' Joshie bristled. 'I plenty God damn nice!'

'Of course, you are. An extremely nice girl,' Critch said smoothly. 'But people are liable to think that you're not nice if you use words like, well, shit and ass and—'

Joshie broke in to say that any God damn people who said she was not nice would get the shit kicked out of them. 'An' Old Uncle Ike an' Old Grandfather

Tepaha an' everyone else, they do kickin'! You say, Old Uncle and Old Grandfather not nice? No one here not nice? You tell me that, huh?'

'No, of course, not. But you've been taught better, Joshie. Surely, your teachers didn't teach you such words, now, did they?'

'Ho! Because maybe so teachers God damn fools! They right, an' everyone else wrong, like hell! I tell you somethin', ol' Critch,' she continued hotly. 'Is like so. You with Apache, you by God better talk Apache. You talk Osage'r Kiowa'r Comanche, maybe so lose God damn hair.'

'Well,' sighed Critch. 'I think I see your point, but . . .'

He left the sentence unfinished, tried to divert the conversation to safer ground. 'What's this place up ahead here?' he nodded. 'I don't see any people around.'

Joshie said tartly that there was nothing wrong with his eyesight: he saw no people because the place was untenanted. 'Land worn out, so Old Uncle Ike say let lie fallow. That's why grass an' weeds grow all over hell. Build up land.'

'That's very interesting,' Critch said flatteringly. 'You certainly know a lot, Joshie.'

'But not know how to talk good,' Joshie said sulkily. 'Not nice girl.'

'Oh, now, look,' Critch smiled. 'That's not what I said at all.'

'Did. Say Joshie talk bad. Say Joshie bad girl.'

'But I didn't! I certainly didn't mean it, if I did! Why, I actually think you're the nicest girl I ever met.'

'But not pretty?' Imperceptibly, she reined her horse in close to his. 'You not think I pretty?'

140

'Why, of course, I think you're pretty,' Critch declared. 'You're an extremely pretty girl, Joshie.'

' 'Stremely? What is 'stremely?'

'It means very – very, very pretty.'

'Well . . .' Joshie fidgeted with her reins, her eyes downcast. 'You like me plenty lot, ol' Critch?'

'I do! I certainly do!'

'How much you like?'

'Well, uh, a great deal. I mean, very much.'

' 'Stremely much?' she said softly. ' 'Stremely, 'stremely much, ol' Critch?'

And she raised her small round face to his, pink lips tremulously parted against the small white teeth. And her full breasts swelled with shuddery sweetness, the nipples firmly outlined against the cloth of her shirt. And her arms went out and up, started to pull his head down to hers. And—

And her horse, brought too close too often to Critch's, curled black lips back from its teeth, and bit the other animal on the neck.

Happenings after that came too fast for Critch to follow.

His horse screamed, side-stepped and stood straight up on its hind legs. It brought its forefeet down again with spine-rattling force. It kicked, bucked and took off across the countryside like a black rocket. Critch had lost the reins at the outset, was now without any control. He could only cling to the saddle pommel and pray – activities at which he was almost wholly unpracticed. And he was given no time for a refresher course.

The horse soared over the five-foot wall of a crumbling rock corral. Effortlessly, it sailed above a startled covey of up-flying quail. It leaped a broad creek bed and a prairie-dog village and an evil cluster of thorn-bush, and an endless number of equally fearsome hazards that lay in its self-appointed path. Fearlessly, it went over them all – a steed with wings on its heels, undaunted and seemingly undauntable. And then it came to a patch of bare earth – a patch approximately double the size of a man's palm. Only a tiny segment of barren soil, hardly enough to see amidst the lush overgrowth. But the horse saw it, and, by some strange quirk of equine reasoning, saw it as a monstrous menace.

The animal abruptly dug in with all four hooves, coming to a split-second stop. Critch locked his boots in the stirrups, and clung to the saddle fore and aft. So despite the tremendous forward thrust, he managed to stay in the saddle. Unfortunately, the saddle did not stay on the horse.

There was a *rip* and a *snap*. Then, the circingle (belly-band) parted, and Critch shot onward and upward.

At the height of his flight, the saddle turned slowly, his feet still snagged in the stirrups, until it was above him. Then he plummeted to the earth with its forty-pound weight on top of him.

The shock of the impact drove a yell from his body. Blending with it, he heard a distant scream from Joshie.

Then he heard nothing.

b

While their horses grazed along the grassy brookside, Kay and Arlie shared their noon meal of soda-biscuits and dried beef. Arlie's normal good humor had returned; was heightening now as he filled his stomach with food. Knowing that his mood was as

142

good as it would be that day, Kay forced herself to confess the deed she had done that morning. An act that she had regretted almost from the time of its commission.

'I sure plenty sorry, ol' Arlie,' she said tremulously. 'Jus' mad and worry about you, or I no do such stupid thing.'

Arlie nodded absently, stuffing a whole biscuit into his mouth. 'Well – *whuff* – well,' he said, spitting crumbs. 'Can't say as I blame you for that.'

'You sure?' Kay said, her tone a mixture of hope and disbelief. 'Was all right to cut bellyband on Critch's saddle?'

Her husband's head moved in another idle nod, and he added a hearty smidgeon of beef to the mixture in his mouth. Sure, it was all right, he said. After all, what was wrong with—

He coughed, choked. Stumbled to his feet bent over, coughing and gagging and spraying the air with soggy samples of his luncheon. Watery-eyed and breathless, he at last rested, turning a terrifying gaze upon his wife.

Kay shrank back from him, her voice a frightened whimper.

'I sorry. I so sorry, nice ol' Arlie. You – you like good col' drink o' water, yes? I get right away!'

'No,' said Arlie tonelessly. 'You stay right there.'

'But – I say I sorry, ol' husband!' Kay insisted. 'I do damn stupid thing, plenty God damn sorry!'

'Huh-uh.' Arlie slowly shook his head. 'You just think you're sorry. If Critch gets killed or hurt bad you'll know what bein' sorry means. You an' me both will.'

'Both? How you mean, both?'

'How I mean, both?' Arlie mocked her bitterly.

'What you think I mean, you God damn stupid squaw? Who the hell you think's gonna get blamed for cuttin' that belly-band?'

'But I take blame! I tell truth!' Kay protested; and then, recognizing the worthlessness of such an admission, she broke into helpless tears.

'That's right. Bawl your God damn head off!' Arlie snarled. 'That helps a hell of a lot!'

Kay sobbed again that she was sorry. She repeated it over and over, adding with humble hopefulness that she was ver' mean, bad ol' squaw and utterly deserving of dire punishment. 'You beat my ass good?' she pleaded tearfully. 'Will make all right, ol' husband?'

'Like shit, you stupid squaw!'

'P-Puh-puhleeze,' begged Kay, fumbling with the belt of her trousers. 'Please spank ass, make every-t'ing hokay again!'

Weeping, her small head bowed, she released the belt clasp, allowed the pants to drop down around her ankles. She raised the short undershift with her hands, completely exposing the curved, tawny-skinned area below her navel.

And stood there crying as though her heart would break. Sobbing helplessly but hopefully, still hoping that Arlie would 'make hokay'. A child in a woman's body. A child environmentally forced into woman-hood.

And at last Arlie's arms went around her, and he called her his ol' squaw with gruff tenderness, and ordered her to stop crying before she got her socks wet.

'You want folks t'think you pissed in 'em?' he teased her lovingly. 'Why, God damn, they're liable to think you're still a papoose and I wouldn't get to diddle you no more.'

144

Kay sniffed; giggled tearfully. She made an innocently profane response to her husband's jest. Arlie kissed her on the head, his lips brushing the snowy 'part' between her tighly plaited braids. He gave her a single swat on her bared buttocks. Then, he bent down, pulled her trousers back up and firmly refastened the belt.

'Now,' he said, 'I hope you learned somethin' from this, Kay. From now on, you keep t'hell out of my business, get me? I want anything done, I'll do it myself. You just keep your hands off and your mouth shut, or I'll have your ass suckin' wind till it sounds like a train whistle.'

His wife murmured a meek, 'Hokay,' then scanned his face anxiously. 'I be good, you bet. But – will be hokay 'bout Critch? You fix everything, ol' husband?'

Arlie said he would do what he could, his actions automatically being governed by Critch's condition. 'If he's hurt bad, or if he's dead – well, I can't do nothin'. A damn fool would know that the cinch had been cut.'

'No, no, please . . .' Kay's eyes filled with tears again. 'He not be hurt bad, please. Not dead!'

'We'll hope not. I figure on findin' out dam' quick.'

He nodded, turned and strode toward his grazing horse. Kay started after him, but he waved her back firmly.

'You stay here an 'wait for me, ol' squaw. Don't want you mixed up in this any more than you already are.'

'But maybe so you need me. Maybe so I tell Critch I cut bellyband, he not be mad at you.'

'Maybe so nobody tells him nothin'.' Arlie said

flatly. 'Maybe so I don't even talk to him.'

Kay stared at him, her head cocked puzzledly. 'How come this? We don't 'pologize, say plenty God damn sorry, ol' Critch he tell Old Uncle 'n' Old Grandfather. You 'n' me be in plenty much trouble!'

'You're gonna be in plenty anyways,' Arlie advised her. 'You an' Joshie both. Paw an' Tepaha sees them scratches on your faces an' find out you been fightin', you're really gonna catch hell!'

'Don't mind that. Not too bad that trouble. But when Ol' Critch tells 'bout—'

'Suppose he *don't* tell about it? Suppose he keeps quiet, an' makes Joshie keep quiet?'

'S'pose?' Kay frowned worriedly. 'S'pose dog shit watermelon? Makes no God damn sense.'

Arlie said that maybe it didn't make any sense to a squaw who was all ass and no brains. But it would make plenty to a smart son-of-a-bitch like his brother.

'And don't you never think he ain't smart,' he added, as he straddled his horse.

'He's not's smart as you!' Kay declared loyally. 'My ol' Arlie, he smartest son-of-a-bitch in world!'

Arlie shrugged off the compliment, wheeling his horse around. 'Don't make up your mind too fast,' he told her. 'Wait and see what I do if Critch happens to be dead.'

c

The four men had ridden the morning east-bound train through King's Junction, debarking from it at the third whistle-stop beyond. From there, via handcar, they had ridden westward again, finally stopping at the point where they were now.

146

One of the men was a section-crew foreman, another a division superintendent of the railroad. The other two were United States Marshal Harry Thompson and his nephew, Deputy Marshal James Sherman Thompson.

The four lifted the handcar from the track, and set it down on the right-of-way. Then they walked down the embankment to a point marked by a heavy staked-down tarpaulin.

'Hope I didn't mess up nothin' by doin' that,' the foreman said anxiously, nodding towards the canvas. 'But one foot was startin' to poke out, an' I figured—'

'You did the right thing,' Marshal Thompson assured him. 'Now, you say you made the discovery about seven last night?'

'Yessir. After the men had put in their hours. I was back-checkin' on a day's work . . . I always do that, Mr. Hardcastle' – a glance at the division superintendent, who nodded approvingly. 'I was coasting along slow, and there was still a little sunlight, so off in the weeds there I get the glint of something bright. O' course, I figure that one of my damn fool hands has left a tool behind . . . I always watch out for tools, Mr. Hardcastle. I know tools are expensive, an'—'

'So is time,' Marshal Thompson said drily. 'Suppose we use no more of it than we have to. Satisfactory?'

'Well – well, sure. I mean, yes, sir.'

'Thank *you*. I gather then that you were alone when you discovered the body, correct? And you have told no one else about it. Very well, then. That leaves us but one thing to do, at the moment. A rather unpleasant chore. Gentlemen, if you will don your gloves and give me your assistance . . .'

. . . The body was rolled into the tarpaulin,

placed on the handcar and transported back to the starting point of the morning's expedition. They loaded it into the coffin that was waiting for it on the evening's west-bound train, and the marshal and his deputy nephew took the same train back to El Reno.

Deputy Thompson had a number of questions and suggestions for Marshal Thompson as they rode through the night. Marshal Thompson, after a considerable silence, had a single suggestion for Deputy Thompson: to shut up or leave their stateroom.

The young man promptly stood up. 'Sorry,' he said stiffly. 'I didn't mean to offend you.'

'Oh, sit down, sit down,' sighed his uncle. 'Don't be so quick to get on your high horse, Jim. If you want to continue in public office, you'll have to remember two things. Touchiness is a luxury you can never afford; that's number one. Secondly, you'll never make yourself popular by telling a man something he already knows, and asking him questions he can't answer.'

'I didn't realize I was doing that. Not that I look upon myself as a participant in a popularity contest.'

'But you *are*, Jim. You most certainly are. I'm both judge and audience in the contest, and the moment you cease to be popular with me, I declare you disqualified.' He gave his nephew a lengthy look, his dark eyes gradually becoming thoughtful. 'I'm joking, of course, Jim; no one, relative or not, has to cozy up to me to hold his job. In fact, it would be the quickest way he could lose it. But I do think it's time you were moving on to something else – something better.'

Deputy Thompson gave his uncle a steady stare; at last, turned it toward the window and the dark panorama beyond. There was the clangor of bells, a blur of red and white lights as they rattled through a crossing. The engine whistled eerily, fearfully, as its headlights swept the prairie and found nothing but emptiness.

'I'm thirty years old, Uncle Harry. I don't have much time left to start carving out a career . . .'

'How true,' his uncle said solemnly. 'In another year or so you'll be tripping over your long gray beard. Wait, now, wait!' he laughed, holding up a hand. 'I mean to see you started on a career, Jim. I mean to do just that. So if you'll stop getting huffy, and listen . . .'

The Territory had been first thrown open to settlement in 1889, he pointed out. (The Territory, as opposed to Old Oklahoma, on the east, which had been moved into some fifty years before by the Five Civilized tribes.) But Deputy James Sherman Thompson had actually seen very little of it, his movements being limited by his job, and that little had become so heavily populated – relatively speaking – as to limit opportunities for a bright young man. Such a man could do well to hie himself elsewhere, to the Big Pasture country, or the Unassigned lands, or one of the other areas recently opened to settlement or soon to be opened.

'Now, the spot I have in mind for you, Jim, is down in the Kiowa-Caddo-Comanche country. I can line up a number of people who will help you there, and with your experience as a deputy marshal and your ability to make friends – How the hell do you make them anyway, Jim? I'm always amazed that anyone as stiff-necked and opinionated as you could have even one friend.'

Deputy Thompson denied that he was either

149

stiff-necked or opinionated. He did, however, have certain beliefs, and he could not, in all honesty, refrain from letting them be known to those who – having lacked his advantages – might hold contrary and erroneous views.

'As for making friends, I suppose it's simply a matter of liking people. I've met very few men that I couldn't find some good in; something that I could honestly like. I like them well enough to remember their names, and the names of their wives and children, and—'

'And,' the marshal nodded his understanding, 'that's all you need to do, to shine the light of recognition upon a world of strangers. I doubt that there lives a man with soul so dead that he doesn't pray for deliverance from anonymity.'

His nephew's blue eyes lighted up with appreciation; he threw back his head and laughed, a laugh so utterly ingenuous and wholesomely good-humored as to warm the marshal's pragmatist's heart.

'Jim,' he said. 'Dammit all, Jim . . .!'

'Yes, sir?'

Marshal Thompson hesitated, started to speak, shook his head. After a time, he said, 'Getting back to the subject of the Kiowa-Caddo-Comanche country, I think the sooner you're down there the better. My friends will give you all possible assistance. With their help, your peace officer's experience and your talent for making friends, you should be a shoo-in for sheriff when the county government is set up.'

'Sheriff?' His nephew was disappointed. 'I'm qualified to practise law. Why not county attorney?'

'Two reasons. You're qualified to practise law, but you've never practised. And an experienced and popular young lawyer, Al Jennings, wants the job.'

'Oh,' said the deputy flatly. 'Oh.'

'You don't like Al? Too many freckles for you?'

Deputy Thompson frowned, brushing the jest aside. 'I can't trust him somehow. He seems, well, too personally involved with his clients. Too intrigued with them. You can't spend much time with him without his talking about how smart such and such a criminal is, or how much "easy money" he got away with.'

'Mmm. So?'

'Well . . . I mean, look at it this way. We both know former outlaws, men who held up banks and robbed trains, who became peace officers. It seems possible, then, that a peace officer – a county attorney – could turn outlaw. Be a bank-robber or hold-up man.'

'A grim prospect for Al,' Marshal Thompson said gravely. 'But a unique experience for you. You'll be about the first sheriff in history to arrest his county attorney.'

Young Thompson grinned half-heartedly. Murmured that the unhappy precedent could be avoided if he became county judge, instead of sheriff. His uncle advised him that the judgeship was already nailed down by a mutual friend who was also an experienced jurist. The deputy expressed dismay.

'He's just not qualified, Uncle Harry. I don't know how he's managed to stay on the bench this long. Why, I've repeatedly heard him advise juries that a reasonable doubt is a doubt you can give a reason for!'

'Well? What's wrong with that?'

'He'll find out if he ever comes up against a truly

gifted attorney. Someone like Temple Houston. It's a reversible error. Anyone ever convicted in his court will get a new trial for the asking.'

The marshal grunted noncommittally; then, his memory stirred, he chuckled, stating that nothing which Temple Houston could do would greatly surprise him.

'I remember a case of his years ago. A dance-hall chippy who'd swindled a bank for practically all its assets. Well, the evidence was all against her; Temple hardly bothered to put on a defense. But, of course, he hadn't thrown in the towel. Ordinarily, this woman dressed to show everything north and south of her navel, but Temple kept her dressed in a sunbonnet and an old mother-hubbard. And when it came time for his summation to the jury, well' – Thompson laughed, 'I wish you could have been there, Jim. I can't remember everything he said, only the concluding words as he pointed from this chippy to the witnesses for the prosecution. "Who are you going to believe, gentlemen of the jury? I ask you, who are you going to believe – this poor old woman, who stands on the crumbling precipice of eternity, or that blood-sucking octopus with its tentacles in Wall Street and its teeth in the throat of our tortured citizenry – *The First Territorial Bank of Pumpkin Wells, Oklahoma!*" The jury brought in a not guilty verdict without leaving the box.'

Deputy Thompson chuckled appreciatively. The marshal recalled another Temple Houston incident.

'It was late in the afternoon, and Temple had been looking pretty wan all day. Right in the middle of cross-examining a witness, he turned to the judge and asked for a thirty-minute adjournment. His honor naturally wanted to know the reason for the request. Temple said it was to preserve the dignity of the court. "I have such a terrible hangover, sir, that only a few quick drinks will save me from flying apart, creating such an unholy mess in these hallowed precincts that even the Blind Goddess must become aware of it, and, lifting her robes, flee in terror."

'Well, his honor pursed his lips judiciously, and glanced at the county attorney. "What say the people?" he asked.

'"May it please the court," the prosecutor said, "the people's concern for the dignity of the court is second only to our sympathy and admiration for our illustrious opponent-at-law. We will be happy to concur in his request for a recess, and even happier to join him for a drink."

'"So will I," the judge said. "Adjournment granted." The three of them went across to the saloon together, and—'

'Uncle Harry,' said Deputy Thompson, '*Uncle Harry.*'

' . . . and then they – Well, what is it?' Marshal Thompson frowned grumpily. 'You interrupted a very good story.'

'I'm sorry. I just wanted to say that I'll be very happy to take the job as sheriff. It should be an excellent stepping-stone to higher office.'

'Stepping-stone? It's an important job in itself.'

'I'm sure you're right, sir. And I'd certainly give it my undivided attention as long as I held it. But—'

'I know, I know,' the marshal gestured irritably. 'You aspire to higher office. The very highest in the country, correct? Now, don't sit there looking lofty. And, for God's sake, don't tell me that any man can be president!'

'Why not, Uncle Harry?' His nephew was honestly puzzled.

'I'll ask you a question. What is the male population of the United States, and how many of those males may simultaneously occupy the office of president?'

'Well . . . there can only be one president at a time, of course, but—'

'Correct, only one, despite the fact that there must be many, many others equally well qualified among the multi-million population of males. You worry me, Jim,' – Marshal Thompson shook his head troubledly. 'I'm afraid my favorite niece-in-law, your dear mother, did you a serious disservice in your childhood. She should have taught you more arithmetic, and dwelt less on the fact that Abe Lincoln was her fourth cousin.'

'*Second* cousin. After all he would hardly have performed the marriage ceremony for a mere fourth cousin.'

'Second cousin, eh? And Mr. Lincoln married her to your father? Interesting, very interesting. There seems to have been a remarkable improvement in your mother's memory, or mine has abandoned me completely.'

'After I serve as sheriff,' said Deputy Thompson firmly, 'I shall run for Congress.'

'Oh, shut up,' said his uncle.

'You introduced the subject of politics, sir. I was trying to discuss the murder of the Anderson woman, Little Sis, that is—'

'How do we know it was Little Sis? How do we know she was murdered?'

'Well . . . of course, we can't make positive identification. But it would certainly seem a safe assumption that the dead woman was she, and that—'

'We can assume that, yes. We can also assume that she was murdered by her older sister. Little Sis jumped the train when she discovered that Big Sis was following her. The latter went right out the window after Little Sis, who she thought was carrying the loot from their many murders – *and she may have been carrying it, Jim*. Big Sis may have gotten it all back from her before beating her to death.'

'But Little Sis couldn't have had the money! Critchfield King had stolen it from her!'

'Did he?'

'Of course, he did! And Arlington King stole it from him.'

'Did he?'

'Yes, certainly! You know he must have, Uncle Harry! Why – why, everything points to the fact that—'

'It points to it, in our minds. Which way it would point in the minds of a jury is something else again, as you should know better than I. Or didn't you tell me you were a qualified attorney? No, Jim,' the marshal averred firmly. 'We have no evidence to go on at all, at this point. Not one whit of proof. We can assume certain things, and I think our assumptions may be correct. Whether we can prove it or not depends on Big Sis.'

'On *her*? How?'

'Quite simply. Assuming that Big Sis was on the train with her sister and Critch King, she must have gotten a good look at Critch. Enough to recognize him if she ever saw him again. Also, she may have found out who he was from someone on the train.

Or, if he was using his right name, she could have gotten it from Little Sis before pounding her to death. In other words, assuming that Critch did steal the money, Big Sis will probably try to get it back from him.'

Deputy Thompson leaned forward excitedly. 'You think she's still in the area, then? Why don't we organize a search party and hunt her down?'

'Hunt exactly where? She could be any place within a fifty mile area. We could possibly dig her up if we had enough time and money, but that would still leave this job half done. Critch King – and, Arlie, too, perhaps – is guilty of being an accessory. The only way we can get him, or them, is through her.'

'I see,' the deputy nodded. 'You'll keep a watch on Critch, and when she tries to make contact with him . . .'

'Right,' the marshal said. 'Right, Jim. And now as your relative and friend, I again implore you to drop your preposterous political aspirations.'

'Sorry,' his nephew said shortly. 'I see nothing preposterous about them.'

'But you *must*! Territorial Oklahoma is governed by appointed Republicans. The state, however, will be Democratic. It's geographically southern, and the settlers are mainly southern, so it will go into the Democratic column. You can overcome that handicap as a candidate for local office, sheriff, that is. You'll have the opportunity to meet people at first hand, to get to know them and become friends with them. And that's all you need to do. But if you run for Congress or the Senate, where it's largely a matter of speech-making and impersonal contact . . .' He broke off, studying his nephew's adamant express-

156

ion. 'I know what I'm talking about, Jim. It's my business to know these things. I can even tell you who your opponent would most likely be in a congressional race.'

'Very interesting,' said the deputy.

'His name is Gore. Keep it in mind, you'll be hearing it for years to come. He's a southerner, a gentleman and a scholar. He's also blind – which will get him a huge sympathy vote, even though he doesn't need it or want it. Don't tangle with him, Jim. He'll beat your pants off if you do.'

'I doubt that, sir.'

'Do you,' Marshal Thompson asked, 'doubt the existence of the word, nephewcide?'

'I don't think I've ever heard of it, sir.'

'Hmmm,' said his uncle ominously. 'Hmmm.'

Author's note: After three terms as sheriff of Caddo County, Oklahoma, James Sherman Thompson ran for Congress against Mr. Gore. Thompson's three-car campaign train carried a banner on each car, the three spelling out his full name. The brass band accompanying the train played *Marching Through Georgia* at each stop. Inevitably, Thompson suffered a smashing defeat, one which, by association, reflected disastrously upon his uncle. Recovering from the debacle after several years, they were powerful political figures in Oklahoma for almost two decades. And several towns in the state bore some form of the family name; for example, *Jimtomson*.

The fictional Anderson sisters had their real-life counterpart in the Bender family, operators of a murder-for-money roadhouse in southern Kansas. Like Big Sis and Little Sis, the Benders are said to have fled into Oklahoma Territory, successfully eluding a pursuing posse and eventually becoming highly respected citizens of the new state. According to another story, however, the posse lied in reporting that the family had escaped. Actually (or so the story goes) the Benders were caught and killed by their pursuers, who then appropriated their ill-gotten wealth for themselves.

The anecdotes concerning attorney Temple Houston are basically true. A reasonable doubt is not, of course, 'a doubt that you can give a reason for'. In so advising juries, the judge in question (we mercifully omit his name) committed a reversible error – one which secured new trials for approximately half the Territorial prison population.

Al Jennings, first county attorney of Caddo County, Oklahoma, ended a most promising political career, by turning outlaw. He showed little aptitude for his new vocation – the entire loot from one train robbery consisted of a bunch of bananas – and other hootowlers jeered his wild tales of gun-battles with lawmen. (His one battle seems actually to have been with a low-hanging tree branch, which knocked out several front teeth.) In a more enlightened era, Jennings might have received the psychiatric treatment which his erratic behavior so clearly dictated. In early day Oklahoma, however, prison was the one place for criminals. And the freckle-splotched former attorney *was* a criminal, by his own admission if nothing else. While in prison, Jennings gained a sad sort of fame by recounting his 'exploits' to a widely read writer. In actuality, the one man seriously hurt or deprived by Jennings would seem to be Jennings himself.

The King ranch, and the town of King's Junction, with its various appurtenances and enterprises are strictly the product of the author's imagination. Completely fictional, also, are the people who populate the town and ranch, including the Kings themselves. Anyone even vaguely familiar with Oklahoma history will know that such places and people did not and could not exist. Anyone not thus familiar will have to accept their non-existence on the word of the author, the son of James Sherman Thompson.

d

Aching in every bone, Critch lay on a bunk in the abandoned farmhouse, his mattress a pile of grain sacks, his covering the blanket from his horse. He didn't seem to have broken anything, though how he had escaped a fractured neck was miraculous. Joshie bent over him, gently brushing the hair back from his forehead, asking anxiously if he was sure he was all right.

'I'll live.' Critch managed a smile. 'Nothing worse than a bad jolting. I just hope you didn't hurt yourself in lugging me in here.'

'Ho!' Joshie dismissed the notion. 'I God damn plenty strong squaw. Strong like hell, by God!'

He smiled at her, laughed softly. She looked away abashedly, eyes downcast. Very carefully, spacing the words out, she said, 'I . . . am . . . very . . . sorry. I . . . do . . . not . . . talk . . . good.'

'Joshie,' said Critch, 'Joshie, dear, I like the way you talk. I wouldn't change a word of it for the world.'

'You – you really mean?' Her wide-wide eyes searched his face. 'No shit?'

'No shit,' he said warmly. 'I like everything about you.'

He meant it. For a momentary eternity he had been dead; he had met death face to face, and the look and smell of her had terrified him.

And now, mercifully, thanks to luck and Joshie's prompt ministrations, he had been brought back into life. Joshie had intervened as death clutched at him. Joshie would provide whatever was needed to complete his rescue.

Like her? Like was hardly the word. He would have loved her if she had been half a ton in weight,

159

with a face as homely as a mud fence.

Smiling, he held out his arms to her: one of the few entirely sincere acts of his misspent life. He drew her face down against his, feeling the soft breasts press upon his chest, feeling the wild pounding of her heart. With incredible gentleness – so gently that he was hardly aware of it – she slid a leg across his body, then drew up the other leg. And was at last in the bunk with him; was lying on top of him.

Unwillingly, he tried to protest, and found her mouth covering his. The protest died in his throat; and she raised her body slightly, one of her small quick hands busying itself with her trousers. The hand finished its task, gave a single swift pull at the fly of his levis. Then, she had settled down upon him again, the small soft-hard body pressing harder and harder. It began to jerk, in epileptic rhythm, delicately fitting itself into and around his own body. And her lips whispered frantically, ecstatically pouring out a stumbling stream of innocent lewdness.

And the soft moistness caressing his crotch. And the bared buttocks filling his hands. And—

'Holy God!' He let out a yell. 'What the hell is this?'

He gave her a shove, almost yelling again at the sharp stabs of pain which the action induced. Joshie flew out of the bunk, stumbling in her lowered trousers and sat down hard on the floor.

She came to her feet, slowly pulling her pants up and fastening them; frowning at him more in wonder than in anger.

'Why you do, ol' Critch? You say you like me.'

'*Why*? Why, God damn it –' He caught himself. 'Well, I do like you, Joshie. I mean it, I like you very much. That's why I couldn't let you do this.'

160

'Is *why*?'

'Of course. When a man likes and respects a girl as much as I do you, well, uh, he doesn't do that to her. Or let her do it to herself.'

'No?' Her head tilted puzzledly to one side. 'He only fock girl he don't like?'

'Uh, well, no, I don't mean that exactly. You see, uh –' he hesitated. 'You see, it's like this, Joshie. Nice girls aren't supposed to have relations with a man unless they're married to him.'

'No want relations. Just fock. Anyway, maybe so sometime we get married, I betcha.'

'Well, uh, yes. Maybe we will sometime. But—'

'Sure t'ing,' said Joshie with utmost certitude. 'King blood got to mix with blood of Tepaha. Is way it is.'

Critch wet his lips, nervously; mumbled that what she said was undoubtedly true. But marriage was something that lay in their future; just how far he was unprepared to say, since they had grown up in different worlds and he needed time to adjust to this one. Also—

'Also, make no God damn difference,' Joshie declared firmly. 'We gonna get married. Now we what you call engage', so is all right to fock.'

'Dammit, Joshie!' Critch started to rise from the bunk, then flopped back with a groan. 'I – didn't you hear your grandfather this morning? He said you shouldn't say such words.'

'Huh-uh, did not. He say should only be used between man 'n' woman. Anyway, don't want to say words 'bout it; just want to do it.'

'Well, you're not going to,' Critch snapped. 'You might have a baby, for God's sake! What about that?'

161

Joshie let out a derisive, 'Ho, ho! Squaw no want baby, no have baby.'

'Well, just the same . . .' Critch began; and then smoothly altered his tone, placing the issue on a practical basis. 'I've had a terrible fall, Joshie, and it's possible that I've been hurt inside. If it wasn't for that, I'd be more than willing to do what you want. Why, my God,' he avowed warmly, 'I'm probably a lot more anxious than you are. But if I tried to when I was seriously hurt—'

Joshie interrupted with the declaration that she would not allow him to take such a fearful risk. 'You hokay now?' she asked anxiously. 'I no hurt you inside some place, maybe?'

'Not seriously, if at all,' Critch said. 'I'm sure I'll be all right as long as I take it easy for a while.'

'Then you take easy. I make you, by God!' said Joshie. 'Ol' Boz, he get hurt inside, too. Make balls no God damn good. Was mean God damn bastard, anyway, but . . .' Her voice trailed off into silence, her small face falling at memory of the ball-less Boz. 'You my ol' husband now,' she resumed, her tone brightening. 'Same as ol' husband, anyway. We take easy now, make up plenty los' time later.'

Critch complimented her on her wisdom, suppressing an inward twinge of guilt. He had never minded lying – in fact, preferred lying to telling the truth, since it was much more profitable of the two, in the long run, and invariably more interesting. Still, lying to someone who was so easy to deceive, so eager to believe, was hardly a thing to take pride in. Nor was the profit in it readily discernible. So why—

'Joshie,' Critch said. 'Come here.'

Joshie said, hokey, and came immediately. Sank

down on her knees at the side of the bunk. 'What you want, ol' Critch?'

His arms went around her. He drew her close, burying his face in her hair. *I want to tell you something, Joshie. Something very important.*

'Want to tell you something, Critch.' Joshie pulled her head back from his. 'Something ver' important.'

'I want to tell you . . .' He broke off, frowning at the seriousness of her expression. 'Yes? What is it, Joshie.'

''Bout ol' Arlie. He cut saddle cinch on horse. Is why you almos' get killed.'

'B-But –' He stared at her, stunned. 'But how do you – why—?'

'Cinch cut. You want me to show you, by God?' She started to rise, paused as his hand detained her. 'Is true, Critch. Ol' Arlie, he cut.'

'You mean you saw him? And you didn't warn me?'

'Course not,' Joshie exclaimed indignantly. 'I listen outside door this morning while he an' Kay talk. Kay want him to kill you. Arlie say maybe so Marshal Thompson find out, so Kay say fix up nice little accident. You see?' – she gave him an anxious look. 'I don' know nothin' for sure. Not till you have accident an' I see cut cinch.'

Critch nodded slowly, an unreasoning rage growing in his heart. That God damn Arlie! What kind of a rotten son-of-a-bitch was he, anyway? Forcing him to come to the ranch, and then trying to kill him!

How low-down could a man get?

Joshie watched him with grave anxiety, misreading his savage scowl. 'I sure sorry, Critch. Jus' not think he try to do it so soon.'

'What?' he said blankly. 'What are you talking about?'

"Bout why he want to kill you. Ol' Arlie tell Kay no good reason to kill you. Kay say there be plenty reason when you find out money gone. She say you hokay 'long as you think you get money back. But you find out he no have money, you sure 's hell kill him.'

She nodded with grave emphasis, dark eyes concernedly fixed upon his face. He sat quite still, staring at her and beyond her. And slowly his lips curled back from his teeth in a frightful grin.

'Gone,' he said. 'So the money's gone.'

'Uh-huh.' She bobbed her head. 'Arlie steal from you, yes? Was very much?'

Critch's grin widened hideously. He said, Oh, no, no it wasn't much at all. Hardly worth talking about. Why – why—

He began to laugh. He fell back into the bunk laughing, then hoisted himself out of it. Began staggering around the floor, oblivious to the wracking pain of his movements; simultaneously whooping and hollering and weeping.

Not much money. *Not much!*

What a wonderful, wonderful joke! The money was gone, and Arlie was afraid he'd be sore about it; killing mad. Imagine that! For, of course, he wasn't a bit angry. Perish the thought! Arlie might *think* he was angry when he got his head caved in and his ribs carved out and his balls toasted over a slow fire . . . so he'd have to keep laughing throughout the mayhem. Make Arlie understand that it was really very funny.

As funny as permanently stripping a brother of his wealth, and then trying to kill him . . .

'*Critch*! Please, ol' Critch! Don' do no more.' Joshie clung to him frantically, her voice half-

164

sobbing. 'No more laugh, please. Scare me plenty much.'

The red haze cleared from Critch's eyes. His insane hysterics ended as suddenly as they had begun, and he docilely allowed Joshie to guide him back to the bunk. He would not, however, lie down in it.

'I think I'd better sit up a while,' he explained. 'Maybe even move around a little. I'm liable to get stiff as a board if I don't.'

'Well . . .' Joshie gave him a doubtful look. 'Well, hokay, but you no ride horse. I go get wagon for you.'

Critch smiled his agreement, then masked his handsome features with an expression of great concern. 'But it'd be way after dark before you could get back here. I won't allow that, Joshie.'

'Ho,' she scoffed. 'I be all right.' But Critch shook his head firmly, over-riding her with the tenderly playful reminder that she was now his squaw and must do as he said.

'You let Arlie bring the wagon. See that he does do it. Tell him I want to talk to him privately.'

'But he try to kill you!' Joshie protested. 'He get you alone, he try to finish job, an' you too hurt to fight back!'

'Now don't you worry about me,' Critch said, chucking her under the chin. 'I'm feeling better all the time. Anyway, Arlie won't be stupid enough to make two attempts on my life in one day.'

'Well . . .' She didn't think it was a good idea. She saw no reason to take a chance that need not be taken. 'I tell you, ol' Critch—'

'No,' Critch said firmly. 'I tell *you*, ol' Joshie. I tell you to have Arlie come after me alone. So that's what you do, yes? Yes.' He gave her a playful pat on the bottom; stood up and kissed her. 'One more thing, Joshie. That bellyband – the saddle cinch – broke, understand? It wasn't cut; it broke.'

'Like hell!' Joshie blazed indignantly. 'Was by God cut!'

'But you don't say that. You say that it broke. You say that,' he said slowly, letting the words sink in. 'Because if you don't, Joshie, I just might stop liking you . . .'

'*No!* Oh, no, Critch!'

'I might if you don't say what I tell you to do. You just might have to go through life using your finger instead of the real thing.'

'Finger *tabu*,' Joshie said. 'Anyway, no damn good. I do what you say, ol' Critch.'

CHAPTER THREE

a

Some five hundred yards from the abandoned farm house, Arlie lay bellied down in the lush growth of weeds and grass, his nervousness increasing with the passing of each minute. Joshie's horse and Critch's saddleless animal were hobbled in the grownover yard of the dwelling, so obviously the two were inside. But as to what condition Critch was in, Arlie could only guess. For more than an hour now, he had lain hidden and watched the place. Fretting, worrying; profanely praying to whatever powers that be that nothing was seriously amiss with his brother. More than an hour of agonized waiting . . . and he knew no more now than he had at its beginning.

A red fire ant crept inside his boot, seemed to sting him endlessly before he could crush it. A miniscule cloud of gnats discovered him, began a gauzily insane dance in front of his eyes. Refusing to be dispelled or dodged, eventually taking refuge in his nostrils.

The experience left his eyes waterily itching, his nose maddeningly irritated. In the discomfort of the moment, he told himself that he didn't give a damn if Critch *had* broken his neck; it would save some hangman the job, since he was certainly long overdue for such a fracture. In the next moment, however, he was retracting the thought with superstition-born haste. He cared very much about Critch's welfare.

167

Oh, yes; yes, indeed. No one could be more concerned for Critch than he. Nothing would gladden his heart so much as the sight of Critch, alive and in reasonably good condition.

Arlie scrubbed his scratchy nose, rubbed his reddened and itchy eyes. He raised his head slightly, looked toward the distant house. His heart executed a sudden skip-jump, and his broad face broke into a delighted grin.

Critch was stepping down from the door of the cabin, coming out into the yard. He was bent over a little, his movements somewhat stiff, and he limped. But he was certainly very, very far from being dead. He had certainly sustained no very serious injuries.

He limped to the horses with Joshie, waited while she mounted her animal and took the reins of his. He waved to her as she rode away, his horse galloping at her side. Then, he hoisted himself up into the door of the house, and disappeared within its shadow-dark interior.

Arlie lay amidst the weeds for a few moments longer. Debating the wisdom of looking in on his brother, and finally deciding against it. Critch would make no mention of the cut cinch, and he would forbid Joshie to. He dared not mention it, lest stern Old Ike drive him, Arlie, from the ranch – in which case, naturally, he would take the stolen money with him, permanently removing it from Critch's reach.

If Critch ever found out that the money was gone—! But never mind that; worry about it when the time came. All that mattered now was that Critch would make no mention of the attempt on his life. He intended to pass it off as an accident. And since an accident automatically cannot be anticipated, a call on him at this point would be awkward to say the least.

How embarrassing to ride miles out of your way to inquire into a man's injuries, when you could have no legitimate knowledge of those injuries. How embarrassing for both of you!

Just wouldn't be right, Arlie thought virtuously. And he began to creep back through the weeds, moving unerringly toward the *arroyo* some half mile distant where his horse was tethered. Essentially a primitive, he could have traveled in this fashion for hours; the hunter who might momentarily become hunted. Instinctively; without conscious effort, his movements were virtually silent. And no telltale wake followed him through the weeds. Now and then his head poked up through the rank growth for reconnoitering, but this was done so quickly, in the fractional second of an eye's blink, that no one could have seen him. Or, rather, realized that they had seen him. At virtually the same instant, he was there and not there. Nothing more, apparently, than a flickering trick of sunlight and shadow.

But while he could not be seen, he saw. And unheard, he heard. So after some eight or ten minutes, he altered his direction, moving off at an approximate right angle to it. After perhaps another ten minutes, he again angled sharply to the right, now heading almost straight toward the house. There was an interval of a few minutes more, and then he came up immediately behind Ethel (Big Sis) Anderson.

She was crawling on her hands and knees, a position which drew her trousers tight over her posterior. Grinning, Arlie aimed a big forefinger at the cleft between her buttocks, and gave her a powerful goose.

Big Sis '*Yipped!*' and reared upward, both hands

grasping at the offended area. Arlie grabbed them, bound her wrists with his bandanna and flipped her over on her back. It was all done too swiftly for Ethel Anderson to follow; before she knew what was happening. One moment she had been creeping toward the cabin. A split second later she was trussed and helpless, and an outside lummox – one of the Kings, apparently – was sprawled on top of her.

He grinned down into her face, pawing roughly over her body until he had found the tightly rolled wad of bills – all the money she had in the world – and her .28 caliber pistol. He tucked the bills into his jacket pocket, and tossed the gun far into the weeds.

Meanwhile, Miss Anderson had considerably recovered her wits, and was much her normal brazen self. 'How about it, big boy?' she said, her eyes sensuously bold. 'As long as you're taking things, why not take me?'

'How I gonna take you?' said Arlie, with assumed idiocy. 'You mean I eat you, or somethin'?'

'Now you just might want to,' she murmured. 'Eat or do the next best thing. Have a look at those tits.'

He pulled her shirt open, studied the pink-tipped abundance that tumbled out. He allowed his mouth to open in wonderment; at last looked up with patently puzzled eyes.

'You only got two,' he said plaintively.

'I only – *whaat?*' said Ethel Anderson. 'How the hell many did you think I'd have?'

'Kinda depends on whether you're a cow or sow or a bitch. Now, I don't figure you for a cow; you're too fuckin' filthy to stay in the same barn with one. So I reckon you must be a sow or—'

'You smart aleck son-of-a-bitch!' snapped Ethel, and she spat full in his face.

170

Arlie grinned, letting the spittle slide down his jaw; making no move to wipe it away. 'You spit pretty good,' he said. 'Want to do it again?'

'You're damned right I do!' she said. And she did. Spitting repeatedly into his face until her mouth was dry, and she could spit no more.

Arlie asked if she was sure she was through; if not, she was to take her time and finish. Miss Anderson shook her head uneasily, attempted an apologetic smile. For one of the very few times in her life she was frightened. Frightened, terrified, rather, to a degree she had never known before. Arlie brushed his sleeve across his face, mopping up the spittle. He continued to grin at her, a meaningless empty grin. A grin that hinted of a bottomless pit, where lurked unspeakable horrors.

Miss Anderson tore her eyes away from the grin; gasped out that she was sorry. 'I mean it! I really am! If you'll just let me go, Mr – uh – Mr—'

'Name's King,' Arlie said. 'The fella you was sneakin' up on in yonder house is my brother, Critch. You, now, I reckon you must be the gal called Big Sis Anderson, and you're plenty wanted for murder.'

Big Sis hesitated. 'All right. But there's probably one thing you don't know. Your brother has the money I murdered to get. He stole it off my younger sister.'

'Mmm? And where's your sister now?'

'Well, I, uh . . . I'm not sure, exactly. But—'

'Never mind,' Arlie chuckled. 'Now I'll tell you something *you* don't know. I stole that money off'n Critch. Took every penny of it an' spent it.'

Miss Anderson nodded promptly; again said, 'All right. You're not going to turn me over to the law, are you? They'd make you dig up that money if you did.'

Arlie said, nope, he wasn't going to turn her in. The Kings weren't much for botherin' the law with their problems, sort of likin' to deal with 'em themselves. 'But you're kind of a problem I don't know how to handle. I mean, what the heck am I gonna do with you?'

'You don't have to do anything. Just lift yourself off of me, and I'll do the rest.'

'You mean you'll just leave? Not come around no more?'

'Why not? There's nothing here for me with the money gone.'

'Now, ain't you nice?' Arlie said. 'I tell you the money's gone, an' you take my word for it just like that. Makes me wonder how anyone as trustin' as you managed to get so much money to begin with.'

'Look!' Big Sis snapped. 'If you've got something to say, say it! Whether you have or haven't got the money it's the same difference. There's nothing I can do about it.'

'There's ain't? Now I'd a thought you could do just plenty about it. You'd sure as hell try, anyways. You'd get the money back, or me'n brother Critch would get a hatchet in our heads. Reckon we'd get one irregardless, what with you kind of havin' the hatchet habit.'

Miss Anderson cursed bitterly and at length, declaring that he could believe anything he wished as long as he lifted his big ass off of her. 'I've told you the truth, God damn you! Now get up before you smother me.'

'No,' said Arlie.

'No? What do you mean no?'

172

'I mean, you ain't convinced me that you wouldn't make plenty of trouble for me an' little brother. So I guess I'll just have to convince myself, won't I? Have to make sure that you don't never come near me or Critch again.'

'Do it then, damn you! But for God's sake get up so I can breathe!'

Arlie removed himself from her, still keeping well down among the weeds. Ethel Anderson sat up, drinking in great chest-swelling gulps of air. Arlie asked her where she had left her horse; learned that it was behind some trees about a quarter-mile to the north. He told her to head in that direction, unbinding her wrists so that she could crawl ahead of him.

They proceeded thus for a few hundred yards, until they had come up on the blind side of the house and were almost out in the open. Then, Miss Anderson suddenly flipped over on her back, simultaneously throwing a handful of dirt in his face and kicking out mightily with both feet. She came to her feet running, racing as fast as her well-curved legs could carry her. She burst out of the weeds and into the open. Heart pounding wildly, she sped toward the trees behind which her horse was tethered. She rounded them, and—

And had to fling herself backwards to keep from being impaled on the blade of Arlie's outthrust knife. He gestured with it, ordered her to stretch herself out on the ground. She obeyed, eyes fixed fearfully on his face. Mumbling incoherent apologies for what she had done. Arlie said genially that she was not to feel bad about it at all. His plans for her had been unchanged by her attempted escape.

'Now, we'll just get you out of them clothes . . .'

He tore them off her with a couple of hard tugs of his hand. 'An' then I'll just cut myself a nice piece of ass.'

Her fear abating, Big Sis said irritably that he could have done that without destroying her clothes. She'd make a hell of a sight traveling across the countryside naked. Arlie said her nakedness would be no bother to her, her mind being occupied by other things.

'Like this,' he said, squatting astride her, and firmly gripping a bare buttock. 'Like goin' around with only one cheek to your ass.'

The cold edge of his knife pressed against the bulging flesh. She gasped, then screamed, as the blade sank in, was almost buried in the pulsing softness.

'What are you—? *No! Stop! SSTOP!*'

Arlie lightened the pressure on the knife, asked what the hell she was fussin' about. 'Just cuttin' myself a piece of ass like I said I was goin' to.'

'You're c-crazy—! *No! N-n-n-noo!*'

Arlie shifted his weight a little, forcing her face down into the dirt so that her screams became a frantic muffled mumble. She squirmed and pitched, and Arlie only brought his weight down the harder, murmuring assurances that she was making a lot of fuss over nothin'.

'What's one piece o' ass to a gal that's got as much as you have? If you're afraid it'll make you lopsided, I can even things up by whopping off the other cheek. Now, you jus' lay real still an'—'

Big Sis reared up violently. Managed one short, strangled scream. Then she flopped down on the ground again in a dead faint; lay motionless and silent.

When she regained consciousness she was lying on her back, her hands again bound behind her. A gag made from shreds of her clothes was in her mouth, and Arlie was seated on her chest, his back to her. He gave her an over-the-shoulder grin; a reassuring wink and nod. Then, taking a tight hold on the loose flesh of her crotch, he brought his knife down hard and slowly inscribed a circle around her uterus.

He had decided to leave her ass intact, he explained, as a relatively harmless part of her body. Instead he was going to remove the real mischief maker. And with her cooperation and his skill, the operation would be quite painless.

'Wish I had me a nickel for every puss I cut off,' he went on, carefully reinscribing the circle with his knife. 'An' ol' Indian trick, y'know, an' us Kings are prob'ly more Indian than white. Funny thing is the woman don't hardly feel it – you don't feel nothin', do you? – till a long time afterward. That's maybe because it's mostly muscle, you know, an' stretchy; got more give to it than a mile o' cat gut. Why I seen a fella stretch a gal's puss clean over her head, an' then let it snap shut around her neck. Man, oh, man, what a sight to see!' His body shook with laughter. 'That gal was flingin' herself around like a chicken with its head off; strangled to death by her own tokus. Now – *lay still!* You keep up that kickin' and squirmin', you'll *really* get hurt . . .'

Big Sis could not lie still; no more could she be silent. Her entire body was racked with involuntary trembling, and an incessant moan came from her muffled mouth.

'Now, less just see,' murmured Arlie. 'Uh-huh, I reckon that'll just about do it. Just one quick pull on the hair patch, an' the thing oughta lift right off as slick as pig shit.'

He knotted his fingers in the pubic hair, gave it a long steady pull. He paused; gave a harder pull. Then turned his head to give her an abashed look.

'You mind waitin' a day or two f'r it to drop off? Seems t'be stuck pretty bad right now. Reckon it musta got sort of scabbed on, what with all the bleedin'.'

He held out his hand, by way of demonstration. A hand that was scarlet, dripping with blood. Then, as her eyes grew wider and wider, he reached around and wiped the hand on her crotch.

'Reckon I oughta put it back where I got it, huh? Well, now that we got that over with . . .'

He stood up, held a hand out to her. She took it silently, staring at him with unseeing eyes, and he drew her to her feet. As he guided her to her horse, helped her to get astride the saddle, he looked searchingly into the frozen face – into the eyes that looked only inward – and was almost shocked by what he saw. Almost moved to pity her.

Almost. He was virtually immune to shock and feelings of pity.

'Now, you're gonna be all right,' he said gruffly. 'You've had the fear of God put into you, an' you figure you're half-killed. But—'

'I know . . .' She smiled at him suddenly; the open, innocent smile of a child. And her voice was thin, high-pitched: a child's voice. 'It's like Papa says.'

'Uh, how's that?' Arlie said.

'I live with Papa,' she piped. 'Papa an' my little sister, Anne. Papa said it would only hurt us at first, and then it would feel good. An' I guess he ought to

176

know, 'cause he's my Papa an' Papas know everything!' She tossed her head in childish bravado; then
her voice clouded, and an incipient whimper came
into her voice. 'But it still hurts. It hurts awful, awful
bad. An' – an'—' Dry-eyed, she began to sob. 'I want
my Mama. *I want my Mama . . .!*'

A bilish lump had risen in Arlie's throat. He
gulped it down sickishly. 'Jesus Christ!' he breathed.
'Jeez-ass Keerist!'

'I got to go now,' said Ethel Anderson. 'You better
go, too, or *your* Papa'll be mad.'

She nodded to him winsomely. Nudging the
horse's flanks with her heels, she galloped away. And
in the dying sunset Arlie stared after her, the naked
woman grown smaller and smaller in the distance.
And at last disappearing, as all things must, at
horizon's end.

Arlie turned, and trudged away in the direction of
his own horse. His big hands clenched and unclench-
ed slowly, and his mind was in turmoil. Emotion-
ally, he was tugged this way and that; self-damned
and self-praised; his inner self simultaneously shaken
and reassured.

Could a thing be both wrong and right? Could
justice be injustice? Condemnation wrestled with
rationalization, and the latter at last won out.

He shrugged as he came up to his horse, his face
and conscience clearing.

'Shit and four are ten,' he mumbled. 'Shot a goose
and killed a hen.'

. . . It was quite late at night when Ethel
Anderson reached the Gutzman farm, and Gutzman
was already in bed. Hearing her ride in, he got up
and lit the kerosene lamp; trying to maintain his
anger with her as she drew oats from the feed shed,

then, after a suitable interval led the horse to the watering trough. There was the sound of the barn door opening, the sound of its closing again. And then, finally, the rasping of weary footsteps, crossing the rutted soil of the barnyard and approaching the house.

Gutzman forced back the beam of approval which threatened to disperse his stern scowl.

So his Greta vas a goot woman. So always she took care of the animals first, herself second. Still, vas such an egxcuse to behave like whoore voman? To stay out half the night, and give him insults instead of explanations.

Standing in his long grayish-hued underwear, he drew himself erect as she entered the door; arms folded across his chest, his expression ominously severe.

'So, Greta!' he boomed. 'You vill now tell me vy – vy—'

The lamp wick was economically dampered, so that there was little light outside its immediate vicinity. His view of her, then, was dim and limited: a head and face, a partial torso, painted upon the darkness. But her nudeness was obvious – the fact that she had been out in public, doubtless before other men, without clothes. And that was more than enough to infuriate him.

'Badt girl!' he shouted. 'Fallen voman! Vy? Vot iss, answer me!'

Ethel bowed her head humbly. Her hands remained behind her, as they had in the beginning.

In her child's voice, she said, 'I lost my thing, Papa. You can't do it to me any more.'

'Vot! *Vot?*' gasped Gutzman, and at last he noted the dark smear of her groin. 'Vot has happened to

178

you, Greta? Vy you talk like leetle girl?'

'I'm my Papa's good little girl,' Ethel said desperately, 'an' my Papa likes my thing bettern' anyone's. An' now it's gone. An' – an'—' She rasied stubborn eyes to his. 'It's not my fault, an' you're not gonna whip me.'

Tell me I'm not, yuh little bitch! Went an' sewed it up, did you? Well, time I tear them threads outta yuh . . .!

'Mein Gott!' Gutzman stammered. 'Ach, my poor leetle Greta! Blease, you tell Gutzy vy – vot—'

'I'm going to kill you, Papa. I'm going to rip your thing off.'

She brought her hands around in front of her, jabbed with the item they were holding. It was a pitchfork, the needle-sharp tines gleaming dully through their encrustations of manure.

Gutzman stood frozen with surprise. Stunned, unable to move, he stammered incoherent inquiries as to the reason for this horror which confronted him. Ethel crept in closer, ignoring his questions; at last beginning to sing:

Jesus wants me for a sunbeam,
A sunbeam, a sunbeam!
Jesus wants me for a sunbeam,
I'll be a sunbeam for him!

She lunged forward suddenly. Gutzman let out a yell, flung himself aside. The tines of the fork sank in the wall behind him, and before he could recover sufficiently to wrest the tool from her, she had jerked it free. Was again jabbing and stabbing at him.

Slowly, he began to back away from her, keeping his eyes on her face. Blindly feeling with his hands for something with which to defend himself. He stumbled against a chair, almost went over backwards as she lunged at him again. He bumped into the stove, cold now after hours of disuse, and began circling it. Too late he remembered the large pile of firewood he had stacked behind it that night. A pile too large for him to move around, or to step over backward. And, of course, he would have to do it backward. Death awaited him the moment he turned away from her.

Now, she laughed with childish pleasure, merrily aware of his predicament: then broke into sobs, declaring her willingness to be a sunbeam for Jesus.

All the time moving nearer. And slowly drawing the pitchfork back for its final thrust.

Gutzman fumbled behind him with sweat-wet hands. Feeling the rough bark of the firewood. Trying to find a stick that would serve as a weapon.

He found none. All were sections of split logs; half-logs, in other words. Too big to be gripped firmly, or swung quickly. Large chunks of wood burned longer than small, though they were often difficult to ignite. Usually, it was necessary to splinter one up for kindling, and—

Gutzman at last found his weapon. He swung with it, an infinitesimal fraction of a second before Ethel could lunge with the pitchfork.

She released the fork, and said a single word; a long drawnout, 'Ohhh,' that was like a sigh of relief. Then, she crumpled to the floor, and there was no further sound from her except for the bubbling of her wound.

Gutzman let out an anguished cry of 'Greta!' He tottered out from behind the stove, and sank down on his knees before her. At first he kept his eyes firmly shut; and when he at last opened them, he kept them turned away from her face and head, from the fatal injury he had wrought, and looked only at her body.

She had fallen on her side in death, one knee drawn slightly up: a semi-foetal position. Gutzman studied the flaring buttock thus exposed, then tenderly shifted her body enough to look at the other one.

He leaned back, frowning. Scratched his frowsy head puzzledly. After a long moment, he turned her on her back, and spread her legs with awkward delicacy. Reaching behind him, he palmed water from the stove's reservoir, splashed it upon her crotch and gingerly scrubbed it with the sleeve of his underwear.

Again he leaned back, baffled by a seemingly idiotic paradox.

His leetle Greta . . . all bloody she was there in the place he had so happily visited so often. Yet how could this be? Where had the blood come from? There was not even the smallest cut, the slightest break in the skin, either there or anywhere else on her body.

He scowled, looking down at her; then suddenly squinted and bent close.

Circling the pubic area, was a deep reddish indentation; much the same kind of marking he had noted on her buttock. He had supposed this last to be a memento of the saddle or of too-tight underpants. Yet that could hardly be, could it, if a virtually identical imprint existed around her crotch.

Gutzman could think of only one thing which might have made such an indentation. One which could not possibly have made it, since, to his way of thinking, it would have been preposterously pointless to do so:

Pressing a knife down hard on the blade's dull edge . . .

Gutzman gave his head a sad shake, firmly and finally denying the ridiculous theory. No one but he was responsible for leetle Greta's death. Only he had contributed to it. He had babbled to her unceasingly, talked until the sound of his voice must have been like the buzzing of bees. And all night long he had pressed himself upon her, taking advantage of her dependency; giggling stupidly at her profane pleas to leave her alone before he wore it out.

How many times had she cursed him, declared that he was driving her crazy. *Oh, Gott, Gott! So sorry I am, Greta!* She had warned him, and he had ignored her. And, now, here was the awful result of his selfishness.

Those curious indentations had nothing to do with the tragedy. Already, even, they were beginning to fade and disappear. They would be gone before the marshal could send someone to investigate, nor was there any point in mentioning them. For he, alone, was guilty. He, Gutzman, that selfish, thoughtless, demanding man, who had made Greta murderously insane, and then split her lovely head with a hatchet.

b

Critch limped out to the well, and drew up a pail of water. He dipped cupped hands into the pail, blew a couple of tiny silverfish from the water and drank thirstily. He repeated the process several times, pausing intermittently to chew down a string of jerked beef. His inner self at last refreshed, he stripped to the waist and gave himself a half bath.

The rays of the dying sun warmed and dried him. He returned to the house, feeling considerably less stiff and achy.

He lay down in the bunk, and lighted a cheroot. By the time it was finished, he was all but drained of his rage against Arlie and was able to think reasonably. To see the dangerous futility of killing his brother.

Marshal Thompson had warned them both about taking the law into their own hands. And the marshal was obviously not a man to be trifled with. He would not accept a murder attempt by Arlie, as an excuse for killing Arlie. He would simply point out that only the law was authorized to deal with criminals, and that individuals who did so were criminals themselves. And that would be that – the next to the last chapter in the life of Critchfield King.

The best argument against killing Arlie, however, was the pointlessness of it. It would not get him his money back. It would leave him stuck here on this debt-burdened ranch, a place he was as incapable of running without Arlie as he was of flying.

There were two good reasons then for not killing Arlie. And added to them, Critch admitted, perhaps a third. The fact that he was doubtless incapable of killing. In the blazing heat of his rage, he had believed himself capable – had sworn that he would take Arlie's life. But now that he had cooled off, had had time to think clearly . . .

Arlie's demise was desirable, of course. If nothing more, killing him was the best insurance against getting killed. For the present, however, it must remain only an ideal. Something only to be achieved if and when the right time came.

In the meantime, and killing aside, Arlie must

certainly be punished. He must be taught that an injury or an attempted injury to his brother, would bring prompt and painful retaliation.

Critch sat up in the bunk, gazed thoughtfully around the darkening room. Then, his eyes lighting, he arose and went over to the stove; reached a hand under it. The hand closed over a metallic object, and he drew it out. Stood hefting a heavy steel poker.

Nice, he thought. Very nice, indeed. And loosening his belt, he slid the poker down his trouser leg. He refastened the belt, took several tentative steps. He could only walk stiff-legged, naturally, but that was all right. Even without the poker, his movements tended to stiffness.

He returned to the bunk. Lay back down again. The darkness became almost absolute, and he closed his eyes. And within minutes was fast asleep.

Several hours later he awakened to the distant rattle of wagon wheels. He sat up slightly to glance out of the window, and he saw the bobbing glimmer of a lantern. He stayed where he was for a time, watching the lantern draw closer, listening to the sound of the wheels grow louder. Then, at a faint *haloo* from Arlie, he arose and limped out into the yard.

'Here!' he shouted. 'All ready and waiting.'

'Good! Be right with you!' Arlie shouted back. And he soon was.

He leaped down from the wagon seat, came forward with anxious offers of assistance. Critch accepted it, directing it so as to conceal the presence of the poker and to place his brother in line for a hard kick as the latter hoisted him into the rear of the wagon.

'Yeeow!' yelled Arlie, clutching at his groin.

'Watch what you're doin', God damn it!'

'Oh, did I kick you?' Critch asked innocently. 'I'm terribly sorry, Arlie.'

'Well, you sure as hell—! Ah, to hell with it,' Arlie said, and he rounded the wagon, and climbed up in the seat. 'Make yourself comfortable on them quilts,' he said grumpily, as they started off. 'Got grub an' a jug of coffee there somewhere, if you want it.'

Critch thanked him warmly. He again expressed regret for the kick, vocally hoping that it had not landed on his brother's balls. 'I know how much that can hurt,' he went on. 'Why, when that saddle came down on top of me today, I thought my nuts had been crushed.'

Arlie cleared his throat noisily. He popped the reins over the horses' backs, sending them forward with a leap.

'Uh, how you suppose it happened?' he said, finally. 'Cinch bust on you?'

'It must have. Anyone who cut it would have to be a real lowdown, rotten, bastardly, mother-jumping son-of-a-bitch – wouldn't he? And I don't know of anyone like that around here – do you?'

'Uh, er, looky,' grunted Arlie. 'Why don't you eat some of that grub?'

Critch said he believed he would, at that, and locating the lunch basket, he began to eat. (He also found the pepper shaker, and loosened the lid on it.) Between mouthfuls of food and coffee, he continued to muse profanely, lewdly and loudly re the type of person – if it were possible for such a creature to exist – who would cut a man's saddle cinch.

'You know what, Arlie? I think anyone who would do a thing like that would screw a skunk in the ass, and then eat its—'

'Shut up!' howled Arlie. 'You hear me, *shut up!*'

'Shut up?' said Critch. 'Now, why should I, anyway?'

Arlie turned around, yelling because, that was why! 'Because if you open your stinkin' mouth one more time, I'll – *Yeeow!*' he yelled and flung his hands to his eyes. '*Eeyow!* You crazy son-of-a – *OOooouch!*'

'What's the matter? You don't like pepper?' said Critch, and began to roar with laughter. 'Suppose you try a little dose of this.'

He stood up in the jolting wagon, raised the steel poker high. He brought it down with all his might, at the very moment the wagon hit a rock and bounced upward. Arlie lurched backwards, the poker almost scraping the tip of his nose. Blinded, he clawed the air frantically, seeking something to cling to. He found it, the poker, that is, just as Critch raised it for another swing. Just as the wagon again bounced high for a second time.

The jounce pitched him heels over head, still clinging futilely to the poker. Also clinging to it, lacking time to let go, Critch soared after him.

They came down between the team, landing precariously on the wagon's swingle-tree. There ensued an insane melee of kicks and punches and gouges, only part of which punished the intended targets, the rest being inadvertently shared with the justly indignant horses.

Angry whinnyings and equine screams rose above the tumult from the brothers. The team reared, and began to race. The wagon literally flew behind them, hitting naught but the high spots; the swingle-tree pitching and tossing like a wild thing.

Arlie and Critch were necessarily and hastily

diverted from each other. As the team tore through a tangle of spiny prairie bush, the one thought of the partially-shredded brothers was to end this man-killing neo-flight. Or, at least, to end their part in it. But destiny apparently had concluded that here were two fools, who didn't know what they wanted and should be given ample opportunity for second thoughts. And the horses had seemingly decided that whatever their whilom masters wanted, *they* didn't want. So they proceeded to blaze a new trail across the countryside – the roughest, most overgrown part of it – taking the brothers King along with them.

Unlike man, however, there is fortunately a limit to the havoc which animals can create. The team reached that limit when they sought to soar over the steep-banked bed of a dry creek. For while they cleared the obstacle themselves, continuing their mad race through the night, they took nothing with them but odds and ends of harness. The Kings remained behind, all-but-buried beneath the shattered wagon.

For a time, they were too battered and benumbed to move. Or hardly to realize what had happened to them. But at last achieving partial recovery, they reached almost simultaneously for their knives – which, of course, had been lost – then, cursed and clawed about for other weapons.

Critch found a wheel spoke, and Arlie found a length of harness chain. They struck at each other feebly, blows which could have caused no more damage if performed with turkey feathers. Panting, they cursed one another, then, exhausted, fell back prone in the grass.

They lay heaving for breath, hearts laboring with exertion. A light breeze rattled the grass and weeds, made a sound of suppressed snickering. A few stars peered down from the blue-black sky, humorously twinkling and winking. From the far distance, space-muted to a near whisper, came a triumphant neighing, a mocking hee-haw . . . the final comment of the fleeing team.

The brothers rested.

They crawled slowly out from under the wreckage. Slowly climbed up the creek bank and out onto the prairie.

They came to their feet. They began to circle slowly, facing one another, their arms outspread. Poised for the advantageous moment. Arlie said he was going to beat the shit out of Critch. Critch said he was going to beat the shit out of Arlie.

'You'll get enough to eat for a change,' he said. 'A nice double helping. Maybe, I'll give you something to drink along with it. Something like lemonade.'

'You smart-aleck-son-of-a-bitch!' Arlie yelled.

'You slimy, sneaky, backstabbing bastard!' Critch shouted.

He suddenly aimed a kick at his brother. Arlie caught his foot, twisted it sharply and threw him to the ground. Critch rolled frantically, trying to get out of the way of what was coming. But Arlie leaped on top of him, and drew a big fist high.

'Now, by God!' he grunted. 'Now, I'm just gonna beat the ever-lastin'—'

He flung himself backward with a howl of pain; began an agonized hugging of his kneecap. Critch mocked him fiendishly, hefting a rock in his hand. He insisted that Arlie's pain was all in his mind, and that such a small rock could not possibly have caused serious injury.

'Have a look at it yourself,' he advised. '*You dirty bastard!*'

He hurled the rock suddenly – barely missed braining his brother. He grunted disgustedly, then brightened as he saw that Arlie was still helpless; ripe for a few hard kicks in the head.

'Now, just you take it easy,' he advised Arlie, his voice hideously soothing. 'Old Dr. Critchfield is going to put you to sleep, and when you wake up – three or four months from now—'

He started to get to his feet.

He sat down abruptly. Grimaced with pain as he clutched his twisted ankle. Wearily, he began to curse.

And Arlie ceased to howl and flop about, and laughed maliciously. 'I hope it's busted, you son-of-a-bitch! Serve you right for jumping me!'

'And I hope your knee-cap is broken! It'll serve you right for cutting my saddle cinch!'

Arlie hesitated, wet his lips nervously. 'About that cinch, Critch. I'll take the blame before I let Kay suffer for it. But . . . hell, you oughta know I wouldn't do nothin' as dumb as that! Maybe they don't have to hide me under a washtub to let the sun come up, but I'm sure too bright to cut a saddle cinch!'

'Then who – you mean Kay did it?'

Arlie nodded with a mixture of disgust and pride. 'The poor damn' nervy little squaw! She was sore, an' she thought she was helpin' me, protectin' me, y'know, an' – well, Jesus! A blind idjit would know the cinch had been cut, and figger me for the fella that cut it!'

Critch studied his brother suspiciously; at last moved his head in a slow nod.

'All right,' he said. 'You didn't cut it. Now what about the money, and don't ask me what money!'

'What mon— All right, all right!' Arlie said hastily. 'I.K. stole the money from you, and I took it away from him. I admit it, if it makes you feel any better.'

'You don't have it now. What did you do with it?'

'Well, uh, what makes you think I don't have it now? Anyway,' Arlie said, defensively belligerent, 'that money wasn't yours to begin with. You stole it off'n them Anderson sisters!'

'Where's the money, Arlie? If I have to guess about it . . .'

'Dang it, Critch, I was gonna tell you later on! After you sort of got settled down.'

'Tell me now.' Critch waited. 'I know you brought it back here from El Reno. What did you do with it after that?'

'I didn't bring it back here. That steel box in my satchel was just to fool you. Wasn't nothin' in it but some cut-up newspaper.'

'All right,' Critch said. 'Same question. What did you do with that money.'

Arlie mumbled that he had spent it. Critch laughed angrily. 'Spent it? What the hell could you have spent seventy thousand dollars on?'

Arlie told him, repeating the information as Critch stared at him dumbfounded.

'What else could I spend it on, with us about to be debted out of the ranch? I spent it on what you're sittin' on. And I don't mean your lousy ass!'

He glared at his brother defiantly. Critch silently stared back at him, his mind in a turmoil. Trying to think. Perhaps trying not to think what the future now held for him. His hand went to his pocket, fumbled fruitlessly for a cheroot. He looked down at himself frowning, seemingly noticing his tattered clothes for the first time. At last he sighed and shook himself; a man coming into reality from a dream.

'What do you think, Arlie? Do you suppose we could borrow some horses around here, anywhere?'

'Ain't likely,' Arlie said. 'These folks work any horses they got, and they'd lose most of a day before we could return 'em. Anyways, you come up on a place out here after dark, you'll likely get shot a-fore you can say howdy-do.'

'I imagine we'd better make ourselves comfortable here then, don't you? Paw will send for us as soon as that run-away team hits town.'

'*If* it hits town,' Arlie said. 'It wasn't headin' in that direction, an' I don't see it as bein' in any hurry to get there. There's too many fields of green corn along the way.'

'Well, then . . .?'

'It's your left ankle that's twisted, right? An' me, I'm crippled in the right knee. So I reckon if we just kind of lean on each other, favorin' our bad legs, an' puttin' our weight on t'other ones . . .'

They got to their feet, loosely speaking. They started to hobble-hop together, and Critch suspiciously drew back.

'Hold up, Arlie! You've got a cut hand!'

'Huh? Well, damned if I ain't!' Arlie said, and he clenched his fist, stanching the flow of blood. 'What's it to you, anyways, little brother?'

'I'd say it was a fresh cut. A knife cut. Which means a hell of a lot to me.'

Arlie said truthfully that it wasn't a fresh cut. He'd

gotten it earlier in the day . . . somehow . . . and it
had doubtless broken open during the recent hectic
events.

'Now, looky, Critch. Just where the hell would I
hide a knife in these rags?'

'All right,' Critch nodded grudgingly. 'Let's get
organized.'

But now Arlie held back, pointing out that a man
who could hide a stove poker in his clothes was far
sneakier than he.

'Shake your arms, little brother. Shake 'em good!
An' maybe you better drop your pants, too.'

'Like hell I will! There's hardly enough left of 'em
to drop, anyway.'

Arlie shrugged; said he guessed he's just have to
risk it.

Critch snorted; declared that he was risking much
himself.

'So don't start anything. If you do, I'll finish it.'

'Same to you, brother Critch. The same to you.'

So at last, they came together, watchfully juxtapos-
ing themselves so that their crippled legs were on the
inside. Then, each laid an arm across the other's
shoulder; and they began the long walk to the
Junction.

The morning was well advanced by the time they
reached it, and they had hardly crossed the tracks
when the train from El Reno arrived. The brothers
ignored it, too weary to look around. Marshal Harry
Thompson descended to the station platform, flick-
ing specks of soot from his snowy white shirt. As the
train departed, he glanced toward the railroad right-
of-way, nodded toward the dark head which poked
up from the weeds. The head disappeared, and

Thompson strode swiftly down the walk toward Arlie and Critch.

He caught up with them a few steps short of the hotel-ranch-house; made affable inquiries as to the cause of their wretched condition. Arlie explained nervously, and the marshal voiced suave concern.

'I imagine you're completely worn out, aren't you? Can't think of anything but eating and getting to bed? Well, gentlemen' – he looked from one to the other, dark eyes suddenly turned crystal-hard. 'I'm afraid such creature comforts will have to be postponed for a while. Indefinitely, you might say. I have some questions to ask you.'

'Uh, questions?' Arlie gulped uneasily. 'Questions 'bout what.'

'Forget it!' Critch said curtly. 'I'm eating breakfast and then I'm going to bed. The marshal can postpone his questions, or do the next best thing!'

'Which,' said Thompson, 'would be what?'

'Go shit in your hat!'

Critch reached for the door. Paused abruptly, hands half-raised, as he looked down the blue-black barrel of the marshal's forty-five.

'That remark you made,' Thompson said, 'became the epitaph of the last man who made it to me. I wonder if you'd like it to be yours?'

Critch shook his head; managed a weak grin. 'I'd prefer to postpone it, sir. Indefinitely, you might say.'

'Or until you've answered my questions?'

'Or until then. But we do have certain rights, Marshal. Before this goes any further, we're entitled to know the nature of your questions.'

'You're right, of course,' said Thompson,

reholstering his gun. 'Please forgive the omission. My questions – to which I expect complete and satisfactory answers – are concerned with robbery and murder.'

c

They were assembled in the hotel's bar room – the brothers and the marshal, Ike and Tepaha. A bottle and glasses of whiskey sat before the two old men. They sipped at it occasionally, their seamed faces expressionless; reflecting not the slightest interest in what was happening or what might happen.

' . . . well, Arlie?' the marshal was saying. 'I'm still waiting. What's your answer?'

'Sure, Marshal Harry, sure. Now, uh, lesse . . .' Arlie wrinkled his brow thoughtfully. 'Just a minute now. It'll come to me in a minute. Uh, mmm, uh – What was that question again, marshal?'

'The same as it was the first fifteen times I asked it! The same as it was damned near an hour ago!'

'Uh, yes, sir?'

'All right, I'll repeat it once more. Three weeks ago, give or take a day, you paid off approximately seventy thousand dollars in indebtedness against this ranch. *Now where did you get the money?*'

'Where did I get it?'

'You heard me! *Yes!*'

'Mmm,' said Arlie. 'Now, lessee . . .'

In the old days, thought Tepaha, there was no interference from men of the law. A bad son was simply reported to his father, who dealt with him as he deemed best. For who was better prepared to sit in judgment than the father, who more able to decide the proper punishment? Surely, since it was the offender who was punished, it was he who should be judged, not the offense he committed. Surely, though errors might sometimes occur, they were much less frequent when the father, rather than the law, passed judgment. This was so, and it could hardly be otherwise. For the father's judgment was of the individual, and there was honor in it as well as knowledge. And the law's judgment was of the faceless mass (and created by that mass) – and this in the name of justice!

At any rate, thought Tepaha, there was no wrong in stealing, except from friends and family. Others who were stolen from were themselves criminal, since, by making their property stealable, they had doubtless tempted an honest man to thievery.

Similarly, it was impossible to defraud an importunate creditor. The worst that could be done to them was not as bad as they deserved. And how could it be otherwise? Trust was not something you gave a man one day, withdrew the next, and re-extended a third. This patently was not trust at all, but rather the most heinous fraud. Real trust was permanent – not something given when unneeded, and taken away when one's need was worst. This was so. Only a law which boasted of its blindness would hold otherwise.

Ol' Marshal Harry full of shit, thought Tepaha.

'For the last time, Arlie,' said Marshal Thompson. 'I'm asking for the last time—'

'I'll answer the question,' Critch said. 'Arlie got the money from me.'

'Of course, he did.' The marshal turned on him grimly. 'I wondered when he or you would get around to admitting it. He stole the money from you, and you—'

'*Stole* it from me?' Critch gave him a wondering look. 'Now, why in the world do you think—' He broke off, bursting into laughter. 'I'm sorry, marshal. I'd entirely forgotten the little joke we pulled on that Indian kid. I guess you must have forgotten it too, eh, Arlie?'

'Now danged if I didn't!' Arlie declared, and immediately began whooping with laughter. 'Don't see how I coulda forgot it neither, the way we had ol' I.K. goin'. Funniest thing you ever saw, Marshal Harry!'

Thompson looked sourly from one brother to the other. 'You expect me to believe that? That it was all a joke?'

'I hardly see how you can believe anything else,' said Critch, 'as long as Arlie and I say it was a joke.'

'Why, sure,' Arlie said warmly. 'You sure as hell couldn't believe I.K. He's the biggest damned liar in the Territory, and they's plenty of people that'll swear to it.'

Thompson said to let it go; whether the money had been stolen from Critch or whether Critch had given it to Arlie was not really important. The—

'Oh, I disagree, Marshal,' Critch broke in. 'The truthfulness of I.K. could be of the greatest importance. After all, if he lied in one instance he'd doubtless lie in another.'

'Forget it!' Thompson snapped. 'All I want to know is where you got that money – almost seventy thousand dollars?'

'Oh, one way and another,' Critch said airily. 'Gambling, cotton speculation; that sort of thing.'

'Can you prove that?'

196

'Naturally, I can't. No one could. Fortunately, I don't have to prove it. However' – he smiled pleasantly, 'I believe I can lend substantial credence to at least one part of my statement, if you'd care to join me in a game of poker.'

Thompson said he didn't care to, or need to. He already knew where Critch had gotten the money: from Ethel and/or Anne Anderson, alias Big Sis and Little Sis Anderson.

'Mmm,' Critch frowned thoughtfully. 'Ethel and Anne Anderson. Now where have I heard those names before?'

'Don't pull that stuff on me, mister! You stole that seventy thousand dollars from one or both of them, *and I can prove it!*'

In the old days, thought Old Ike King, a man did what he was big enough to do, and mostly there wasn't much difference between the men whose necks he stretched or who stretched his, if so it was to be. Mostly there was nothing personal in it, however it was. It was just a case of taking or being taken, killing or being killed. Well, sure, there was fellas that boohooed and whined about it – but there was fellas that would cry if you hung 'em with a new rope. And, sure, maybe you wished things was a different way; but they wasn't, and all you could do was hold out and hope.

In the old days, thought Old Ike King, a friend was someone you wouldn't kill, even when you had the chance, and vicey versa. A friend was someone you'd kill for and vicey versa. A friend was someone who did no wrong, no matter what he did; who saw you as doing no wrong, no matter what you did.

Now the *padres* weren't bad fellas, in their own

way. But it was only natural that they should be mixed up about right and wrong, since they seldom got shot at or scalped, if at all. It was easy for them to believe that there was a fella with a long gray beard who lived up in the sky and looked out for everyone or anyways never let 'em get killed unless it was for their own good. It was easy for them to believe that there was a hell deep inside the earth, instead of its really bein' where you didn't have to dig for it.

In a funny kinda way, Old Ike King and the *padres* really thought a lot alike. They believed that whiskery fella up in the sky wasn't never wrong about nothing, whereas Ike believed that it was friends, those closest to him, who did no wrong.

You had to believe in 'em, see? You'd go out of your mind if you didn't, what with having to decide a hundred times a day what was right or wrong or halfway between.

To come right down to cases, what the hell could you believe in if not your friends and family? A man that would doubt them and believe an outsider would have to be a plumb sorry asshole . . .

'. . . afraid I don't understand, Marshal,' Critch was saying. 'You state that I stole the money from the Andersons, together or singly, yet you don't seem to have any idea of the amount they had. I do hope this isn't normal procedure for you, sir. To draw an analogy, you could charge a man with horse-stealing, with no proof that the horse ever existed.'

Thompson lowered his head doggedly, his face reddening. 'We know this,' he said. 'The Andersons were in business for approximately ten years, during which time they killed close to forty well-heeled travelers. It's not unreasonable to believe then that their aggregate loot amounted to seventy thousand dollars.'

'Maybe, maybe not,' Critch shrugged. 'The sisters had expenses during those ten years. It's not unreasonable to believe that those expenses amounted to forty or fifty thousand.'

'I'm talking about their net loot! After expenses!'

'Umm-hmm. I assume your estimate was arrived at after consulting the various relatives and heirs of the murder victims? They told you the probable amount the deceased had on their persons.'

'Correct. There was one man alone who had more than ten thousand.'

'Yes? And what did some of the others have?'

'Well, there was one with seventy-five hundred, and one with four thousand plus, and another with close to eight thousand, and—'

Thompson broke off, his mouth literally snapping shut. Silently, he berated his nephew for persuading him to venture forth on what was patently a fool's errand.

Critch laughed softly. 'Well, Marshal? If the individuals you mentioned are typical, the sisters must have netted closer to half-a-million than seventy thousand. What do you suppose happened to the rest of it?'

'Don't get smart with me, young man!'

'I wouldn't think of it, sir. You've got trouble enough in store for you, as it is. It's my guess that the heirs of practically every missing person in the country are going to claim that their loved ones were murdered by the Andersons, and that said loved ones possessed small fortunes in cash or its equivalent at the time of their demise. By the time the claims are all filed and adjudicated, to no one's satisfaction, of course, I suspect that you and the people who appointed you are going to have something in common that you don't have now. You're both going to wish you were dead.'

The marshal grunted, silently guessing that Critch was probably right. In any case, he had no intention of finding out by filing charges against young King. There was simply no evidence to support an arrest. No proof that the Andersons had had anything to steal, or that Critch had stolen it.

For his part, Critch was not feeling nearly as easy as he acted. He still could not bring himself to look at his father. Nor had Old Ike spoken a word, or otherwise indicated what he felt. That he must know or be reasonably sure that the money was stolen seemed certain. And whether the law, as represented by Marshal Thompson, could prove it meant nothing to him. Old Ike was his own law. He passed his own judgments.

'Well, Marshal?' Critch leaned against the bar, easing the weight from his injured ankle. 'I believe I've said all I have to say. Do you still want to arrest me?'

Thompson shook his head; said that he'd never wanted to arrest anyone in his life. 'So, no, I don't want to arrest you. In fact, I didn't come here with any real hope or intention of doing so. I'm probably not as familiar with the criminal code and the rules of evidence as you seem to be. But I'm sufficiently versed in them to know when I have a case against a man and when I don't – and I obviously didn't in this instance. As long as I was here, of course, I tried to do my damnedest. But the main purpose of my visit – I believe I mentioned it earlier, didn't I? – is murder.'

'Murder?' Critch blinked. 'What murder?'

'The murder of Ethel (Big Sis) Anderson.'

'But that's cra—!' Critch broke off, made a business out of lighting a cheroot. Gained a few seconds time to think.

There was something wrong here; something subtly out of key in the marshal's attitude and tone. A charge of murder would naturally take precedence over any other, so why . . .? Never mind, Critch thought, never mind. The question was, how to use it to his own advantage. Get himself solidly back in the good graces of his father.

'Well, Marshal . . .' he shrugged. 'Perhaps, if you're going to accuse me of murder . . .'

'I'm not sure that I am going to. Perhaps I'll charge Arlie instead.'

He turned to grin coldly at Arlie, who was gulping a drink of whiskey. Arlie choked, spluttered and let out an indignant howl of denial.

'That's a God damn lie! I did not neither kill that woman!'

'So?' The marshal's brows went up. 'Then if you didn't, Critch did. I know that one of the two of you is guilty. You see, gentlemen . . .'

Big Sis had been killed the previous afternoon, he explained. Killed in the vicinity of the cabin where Critch had ostensibly been recuperating from his injuries. Arlie had also been seen in the area at the time, and, like Critch, had had the opportunity to commit the murder . . . *to which there had been an eyewitness!* However, the eye witness had been some distance away, and he was only sure that one of the brothers had done the killing – not which one. So . . .

'There's no problem here,' Critch said quietly. 'I'm guilty, Marshal.'

'That's an unqualified confession?' Thompson said. 'You wouldn't like to take some second thoughts?'

'Second thoughts? What about?'

'The fact that my eyewitness actually inclines to the belief that Arlie was the killer rather than you. Now, you were right nearby at the time of the murder. You could have witnessed it. And with you to corroborate the testimony of my witness . . .'

'Now, Marshal . . .' Critch gave him a stern look. 'You surely aren't suggesting that I incriminate my brother by lying to you?'

'I'm suggesting that you're lying right now! That you're doing so to protect your brother!'

'Nonsense! Why, I'd have everything to lose and nothing to gain by lying.' Critch shook his head; let it bow with humility. 'As things stand now, I know my father can't have a very high opinion of me. He couldn't possibly consider me fit to carry on in his footsteps. Given time, I might be able to redeem myself in his eyes, but I could only get that time by putting the blame on Arlie for a murder that I—'

'You don't have to put it on me!' Arlie snapped. 'I'm doin' it myself. I 'preciate your tryin' to protect me, little brother, but I ain't gonna allow it.' He drew himself up, extending his wrists. 'Put the cuff on, Marshal Harry. I done that killin'.'

The marshal looked at him, shook his head cynically. He had misstated the facts a little himself, he said. His eye-witness was actually of the opinion that Critch was the killer. So if Arlie would corroborate the witness's testimony . . .

'I won't!' Arlie said doggedly. 'I done it, an' I'm takin' the blame.'

'You didn't, and you're not,' Critch said. 'I'm your man, Marshal.'

'The hell you are!' ⎫
'The hell you are!' ⎬ shouted the brothers King.

And as they squared off from each other, their fists drawn back, the marshal suddenly burst into laughter. Smilingly assured them that neither was guilty, that the person who had killed Ethel Anderson had already admitted it.

'Now,' he went on, 'you have a right to know why I put you through this rigmarole. The answer is that I felt you two were a potential source of very big trouble. And by way of heading off that trouble, I had to resolve some very serious doubts I entertained concerning your character.'

'They ain't nothin' wrong with my boys' character . . .' Old Ike spoke for the first time. 'Asked me, I'd a told you.'

And Tepaha added that ol' Harry was one big damned fool, unable to see what was obvious to an idiot.

The marshal nodded in suave apology. 'Not knowing them as well as you, I regarded them as two very determined, self-seeking young men. Thoroughly selfish and willing to go to any lengths to get their own way, I am glad to say that I was wrong.'

He was by no means sure that he had been wrong. Still, it was a world of miracles was it not? And if giving a dog a bad name turned him bad, perhaps by giving him a good one he could be made – well, safe at least.

'Shit,' grunted Old Ike King; then, with Tepaha, rose heavily to his feet.

He started toward the door. Tepaha trailing;

rambling of plans he had to make and the lack of time for damned foolishness. He added that the boys were to eat themselves some breakfast. Then, after a moment's grudging pause:

'Welcome to stay'n eat, too, Harry.'

'Why, thank you, Ike . . .' The marshal hesitated. 'If you're sure it's not too much trouble.'

Ike gestured, brushing the notion aside, and went on out the door. But Old Tepaha turned, eyes blazing proudly: spoke in a mixture of Apache and Spanish, as do all wise men when both forcefulness and delicacy are required.

'Has a dog entered the lodge of Old Ike King?' he inquired. 'Surely no man would suggest that his host was so poor in manners and goods as to make his presence troublesome.'

'I am no dog,' Thompson replied. 'We have smoked together and been warmed at one another's fires, and we are friends.'

'Then, heed me!' Tepaha said. 'In the lodge of Old Ike King, there is always meat of which any man may eat his fill. Also, there is always drink. Mescal, and tequila, and for honored guests the finest whiskey.'

The marshal inclined his head courteously. 'I have seen this,' he declared.

d

Breakfast finished and farewells exchanged, Marshal Thompson walked back through the village of King's Junction and entered the railroad station. He checked the arrival time of the next west-bound train with the half-breed station agent; then, went down the station platform to its end, and came to a stop behind the freight-shed.

He was concealed there from both the townspeople and the agent. I.K. promptly scampered up from the right-of-way ditch, and joined him. His suit and other garments had been recently purchased but no one would have guessed it from his appearance.

'Twenty-three skidoo, Marshal Harry,' he said pertly. 'How your hammer hangin' ?'

Thompson replied that it had seemed to be satisfactorily suspended at his last inspection. Then, shook his head amazedly as he looked the young Indian up and down.

'My God, I.K.! How can anyone manage to get so many grease spots on him?'

'Ho, ho,' I.K. said, companionably nudging him with an elbow. 'Don' kid me, kid. I a chicken inspector.' Then, after taking a cautious look around, 'You got 'em tied up, huh? Haul 'em to station like God damn hogs?'

The marshal said, no, he did not have the King brothers tied up. And, no – replying to the youth's next question – neither had he shot their asses off. I.K. gaped at him; profanely professed puzzlement and displeasure.

'What kinda shit you make, ol' Harry? That Critch have seventy-two thousand dollars he steal—'

'That he *probably* stole,' the marshal interjected. 'But there's no way of proving that he did.'

'Sure, there is way! If money not stolen, how come he not make 'plaint to you when Arlie make me steal from him? You ask him, ol' Harry. Watch sonofbitch squirm.' I.K. nodded firmly, giving Thompson a speculative look. 'Maybe I better be marshal. Show you how to do job.'

Thompson said equably that maybe he had. As preparation for it, he suggested that the young Indian first learn how to tell the truth – or how to lie a hell of a lot better.

'Critch insists that he gave the money to Arlie, and Arlie agrees that he did. Since they are not proven thieves, and you're an admitted one – and a liar as well—'

I.K. ripped out an indignant curse. 'I never tell lie, by God! Name me one God damn time I lie!'

'Just now, for one. And yesterday afternoon when you had the section-crew foreman send me that telegram.' The marshal looked at him sternly. 'You could have caused some very serious trouble by doing that, I.K. Fortuntely, I got a later telegram from a constable down the line, identifying the man who actually did the killing.'

'Act'ly did it?' I.K. exploded. 'What you mean, act'ly? Ol' Arlie kill her – same damn woman you show me picture of! Stab her to death with knife!'

'No,' said Thompson. 'No.'

'Well . . . I quite some way off. Maybe so make mistake. I see Critch stab her, and t'ink was Arlie.'

'No. You saw nothing of the kind, because neither of them killed her.'

'By God, yes! Yes, yes, yes!'

The marshal said, by God, no! No, no, no! 'The woman was killed last night by a farmer named Gutzman. She'd been living with him for the past three weeks. Apparently, she suddenly went out of her mind, and he had to kill her in self-defense.'

'But – but—' I.K. was suddenly struck by inspiration. 'Hokay, was maybe like this. Ol' Arlie or Critch stab her like I say, partly kill her, then ol' Gutzman—'

'Finished her off?' Thompson shook his head. 'No, I.K. She wasn't stabbed, or even scratched. Her

206

only wound was in the head, where Gutzman hit her with a hatchet.'

'But, by God—'

The youth's mouth opened and closed helplessly. He gestured wildly, pounding his fist in his palm. Again he tried to speak, and again was helpless. At last, he gave up. Fatalistically accepted the paradox of having seen what he could not have seen.

'By God,' he said, looking across the railroad tracks and beyond, into the endless expanse of the King ranch. 'I guess I screw t'ings up good, I betcha.'

'Ah, well,' Marshal Thompson said, 'we all make mistakes. The point is to learn from them, and do better in the future.'

'Ho, boy, some future I got!' said I.K. glumly. 'I stay 'round here, ol' grandfather an' ol' uncle cut my God damn balls off.'

The marshal said that it seemed wise, under the circumstances, for the youth not to stay there. 'Now, you seem to be basically a bright young man. Just the fellow I need for a job in my office . . .'

'Hey, is God damn fine, Marshal Harry!' I.K. exclaimed. 'I wear big badge, shoot people's ass off, yes?'

'We-el, no, not exactly. You'd be my chief broom-and-mop deputy. Have full charge of keeping all the offices clean. It doesn't sound like much of a job, perhaps,' the marshal went on. 'But it would pay you enough to live on, and give you an opportunity to go to school.'

'Humph!' said I.K. 'School!'

'Yes, school,' Thompson said. 'You need it, I.K. Without schooling, an education, I see a very unhappy life for you in Oklahoma.'

I.K. grunted, gave the marshal a sardonic look. For the first time, his voice took on an edge. 'I tell you 'bout Indian in Oklahoma, ol' marshal. What kinda life we gonna lead. Like you say, I smart young fella, so I tell you . . .'

'Yes?'

'No. All I tell you is, I know plenty already. How to gamble, get drunk, screw women. Is all I need to know.'

'How about lying?'

'Lying?'

'You heard me,' Thompson said sternly. 'You don't lie worth a damn, now do you? Why, I've caught you in two lies this morning, and I wasn't even trying.'

'But, dammit, was not – !' I.K. caught himself; fatalistically gulped down his denial. 'Hokay,' he sighed. 'Maybe not lie so damn good. Ol' Critch an' Arlie maybe lie one hell of a lot better, no shit.'

'Well, then.' The marshal spread his hands. 'Well, then, my young friend?'

'Well . . . I learn how to lie good in school?'

'Now, where else would you learn?' Thompson said equably.

'I learn from first-class liar books? Books full of God damn lies?'

'See for yourself,' Thompson shrugged.

'By God, I do it! We shake on it, Marshal Harry!'

He thrust out a grime-smeared palm.

Thompson looked down at it, diplomatically substituted a cigar for his own hand.

'Smoke up,' he said, striking and holding a match. 'To your glorious future as the biggest liar in Oklahoma.'

I.K. exhaled a great cloud of smoke. Gave him a shrewdly knowing grin.

'Don't kid me, kid,' he said. 'I a chicken inspector.'

e

It was well before daylight when old Ike King, after an uneasily restless night, wearily pushed himself up from his bed and began to dress. The month was August and the night had been a scorcher, yet he could not fault the heat for his inability to sleep. Why, hell, heat had never bothered him no more than cold. Not *really* bothered him, that is, until maybe the last year or so. So, obviously, something else was making him feel as he did.

A feeling that old fires had begun to blaze in his stomach; that his lungs were all but choked on the fumes from them.

A feeling that his heart, despite its increasingly heavy pounding, might stop beating at any moment.

He finished dressing, sat down on the bed for a time to rest. He got to his feet again, trudged to the door and went out into the hall.

He and Tapaha met at the stairs, and they descended to the bar room together. Over stiff drinks, they grunted and grumbled at one another, and Tepaha revealed that he also had slept badly. Unlike Ike, however, he had pinpointed the cause.

It was the kitchen squaws. Old age had made them slovenly and careless, so that the best of food became botched in their hands. Consequently, there was such an uproar in a man's guts after eating that the thunder of it made sleep impossible. And he was indeed lucky to be wakeful, since he otherwise might die of the squaws' evil messes.

Ike said he was full of shit.

'Critch's been eatin' their cookin' for six months, ain't he? A swell young fella that ain't never et in nothin' but the finest places. He says the food's fine, an' I reckon he knows more than a stupid old bastard like you.'

Tepaha said Ike was full of shit.

'Shit,' they said in unison, glaring at each other. And they went in to breakfast together.

They ate considerably more than usual – Ike to show his contempt for Tepaha's opinion; Tepaha to show that he was as hardy as Ike.

Then, with Ike's sons and Tepaha's grand-daughters gone on their day's rounds, the two old men returned to the bar.

They had several more drinks, occasionally nodding over their glasses; talking hardly at all. After an unusually long silence, Tepaha said it was time for their walk, and Ike declared flatly that they had just returned from it.

'Tryin' to trick me, huh?' he jeered. 'Think I don't know what I'm doin' no more.'

Tepaha started to voice a profane rebuttal; suppressed it after a sharp look into his old friend's face.

'You too smart for me, Old Ike,' he said; but was not quite able to resist a small jibe. 'Too bad you not so smart with Creek-nigger wife.'

'Hell,' Ike grumbled. 'Bein' a Creek didn't make her a nigger. Ninety-nine to one she wasn't. I was just jokin' her.'

'Sure. I just joke, too,' said Tepaha.

Ike gulped down another long drink, felt a turgid boiling inside him. He passed a hand over his brow, wiping away the cold, oozing sweat, and gradually a sly look spread over his face.

'God damn,' he laughed. 'Damned if I didn't put the joke on her.'

'How? What you say, Old Ike?' said Tepaha.

Ike sat grinning, not answering him.

When he spoke, it was of the good days when they were young, and they had fled a Mexican firing-squad together.

'Kids nowadays don't have no guts no more like we had, Tepaha. Lock 'em up and tell 'em they're gonna get shot in the mornin', an' they'd probably play with their peters all night.'

'Kids no damn good,' Tepaha agreed.

Ike had another huge drink. He needed it to offset the effects of the first one. At least, he needed it.

Tepaha asked him how he had happened to be in Mexico in that long-ago time. Ike said there was nothing unusual about it.

'Reckon I was about twelve when I took out from Louisiana, and into *Tejas*. Didn't have hardly nothin' with me but my clothes an' this old Collier five-shot. You ever see a Collier, Tepaha? Well, they was flintlocks – pistols, and they started makin' 'em about 1810. Don't know whether they was ever issue or not, but this blue-coat had one, an' . . .'

His voice died, but his lips continued to move. Filling in a gap in the story which some part of his mind chose to keep silent. Then, after two or three minutes, he again became audible.

' . . . mission wasn't too bad, but two years of it was all I could hold. They just wasn't anything interestin' goin' on; if it was interestin' the *padres* stopped it, an' them mission Indians sort of rubbed me the wrong way. I mean, what the hell, Tepaha.

What kind of life was it for an Indian to hang around bein' told what to do an' when he could do it. I'm not sayin' the *padres* was mean to 'em, but—'

'Padres should have beat red asses,' Tepaha said scornfully. 'Mission Indians – God damn soup Indians! Sing, pray, maybe so get nice bowl of soup. Shit!'

'Well, that's the way I felt,' Ike continued. 'So I was a growed man, by then, fifteen an' some, so I just took me off into Mexico which was right handy there. Borrowed me one o' the mission horses to start with, an' when it got used up I started borrowin' from the *Mejicanos*. Done some other borrowin', too, like a bit of money now an' then t'spend in the *cantinas*. An' what with one thing an' another, I finally wound up in that jail where you was . . .'

He looked at his empty glass; pushed it aside. He picked up the bottle and drank from it – drank until Tepaha gently took it out of his hand.

'You say you start out from Louisiana, Ike. Was your home?'

'*Florida!*' Ike suddenly shouted. 'Don't you ever remember nothin'?'

'Florida home of Seminole,' Tepaha said. 'Most same as Creek.' And after a silence, he asked, 'You part Seminole, ol' Ike, how come chase across Louisiana?'

He could not explain his curiosity. In all the decades they had been together, he had given hardly a second thought to his friend's origins. But now, inexplicably, the matter had become of great moment to him.

' . . . ain't part Seminole,' Old Ike was snarling. 'Ain't part Creek 'r Cherokee 'r Choctaw 'r Chickasaw. But when they started movin' the Tribes up the trail . . . 'bout 1830 it was for my people . . .'

As before, his lips continued to move, but soundlessly. Omitting that which his mind preferred to keep silent, or which was too painful for telling. But Old Tepaha was able to supply much that was missing for himself.

The Five Tribes had owned much of the richest land in the south. Industrious, inventive, and well-educated, they were increasingly the envy of their white neighbors. And as the white population grew, exerted more and more pressure on Congress . . .

The forced exodus of the Tribes from their homeland was one of the most shameful and least remarked episodes of history. Uprooted, thousands upon thousands, they were herded west-by-north to a wilderness across the Arkansas, where they were to have their own nations and live forever in freedom. They would be 'happier' thus, of course. It was for the red man's 'own good'.

The unwilling migration began in the 1820s and ended some twenty years later. Many who began the journey did not complete it. So very, very many that the route by which the red men made their forced march became known as The Trail of Tears.

The white government generously decreed that the Indians be allowed to take all their possessions with them to their new homeland. Everything – including Negro slaves. And then as now, a Negro was anyone having Negro blood, however infinitesimal the amount might be . . .

Tepaha gave Ike a sharp look – which told him nothing at all, of course. Hesitantly, he said, 'You overseer's boy, Old Ike? Maybe bluecoat's son?'

'Who the hell say so?' Ike glowered. 'What's the difference, anyways?'

213

Tepaha shrugged; said that there was none. 'Just asked, ol' Ike. You say you not Indian. Not Seminole or Creek or—'

'GOD DAMN!' Ike burst into uproarious laughter. 'God damn if that wasn't a joke on her!'

His laughter grew louder, more violent. He began to shake with it, eyes bulging, the veins on his neck standing out. He coughed, gasping for breath, but still the laughter would not stop. His eyes found Tepaha's, inviting him to share in the joke of his heritage – and the impending joke, the greatest jest of all. Then, very slowly, he arose from his chair and drew himself up majestically.

'I am Old Ike King,' he said in Apache. 'Lions flee at sound of my name, and great bears grovel before me and lick at my balls, lest I beat them with a small stick. In my lodge there is always meat, and—'

His heavy body crashed to the floor, shaking the entire building.

The kitchen squaws came running in, crying out with alarm and wonder. But Tepaha stamped his foot at them, cursing terribly, and drove them from the room. For the senseless chatterings of squaws will creep like maggots through a man's ears and into his brain, creating such havoc that his own speech becomes likewise idiotic. This is well known.

Tepaha went down on his knees at the side of his fallen friend. He said, come, Old Ike, it is time now to make plans – and he drew an arm of Ike's across his shoulders, put his own arm around Ike's back. And slowly, an inch at a time, he stood up. Miraculously lifting the dead man with him.

Staggering, knees buckling with the terrible weight, he started for the stairs. For they were brothers, and he was Tepaha, chief *vaquero* for Old Ike King.

He made it to the foot of the stairs, shakily felt for and found the first step. After several attempts, he managed to bring his other foot up on the step. Then, stood there panting, a great rattling coming into his chest; his eyes all but blinded with sweat.

'By God,' he mumbled, his heart thundering like a war drum. 'You one heavy son-of-bitch, Old Ike . . .'

He got his foot on another step, started to bring his other foot up with it. But something had happened to the stairs, something so strange, that he was trans-fixed with wonderment. Could only watch as they slowly became perpendicular, then gradually bent down over him until he was looking up at the ceiling.

From somewhere came the sound of a mighty crash. So great that its echoes seemed never to end. There was a moment of incredible pain, and then bliss such as Tepaha had never believed possible.

'By God, we do it, Old Ike,' he thought proudly.

The kitchen squaws came running in again, and now the clattering of their voices was such as to demolish the brain of the wisest man. But Tepaha had already deafened his ears to them.

Permanently.

Epilogue

The lowest of dogs may piss on the loftiest of dead
men . . .

This is well known.

Arlie commented idly on the fact one fall Sunday
afternoon when the two brothers, accompanied by
Joshie and Kay, visited the last earthly resting place
of Old Tepaha and Old Ike. The two men had not
been buried in the despised fashion of whites – for
why should they? Instead, their fully-clad bodies had
been placed in a comfortable sitting position, then
covered over with rock to form an Indian *wickiup*.
They were thus protected from the teeth of varmints,
but not entirely from the elements, which, after all,
they had lived with all their lives and might need in
death (so far as anyone knew). It was possibly this
last which inspired Arlie's remarks that Sunday
afternoon:

'Heard me a story once about a Osage that was
buried in a *wickiup*. Seemed like he'd owned several
pet bitches an' their smell was still strong on him. So
naturally every damn dog in the Nation come around
to take a piss on his grave. Well, it turned out that he
wasn't really dead at all, just in what they call a state
of suspensive annie-mation, or something, an' all this
dog piss leaked through and snapped him out of it.
He came bustin' out of the rocks, an' went back to
his village. But it was the funniest God damn thing,

216

Critch – you know what happened?'

Critch nodded smiling, having heard the story: no other Indian would speak to the man, or give any sign of recognizing his existence; not even his own wife, when he had intercourse with her. As far as the Indians were concerned, a man who died stayed dead, and this creature who had returned to them was only an evil spirit.

'Well' – Arlie took a critical last look at the graves. 'Just one thing missing, I guess. There ought to be a war spear sticking up betwixt 'em, with a scalp hangin' from the top. Just don't seem right somehow without it,' he added, sidling a glance at his brother. 'Critch, y'wouldn't feel hurt, would you, if I slipped into your room some night an' lifted a little hair?'

'I wouldn't feel hurt,' Critch said. 'But you would.'

Arlie laughed and slapped him on the back. They headed their horses homeward, the two girls following.

As they rode, Arlie spoke seriously to his brother. 'Kinda late to be thankin' you, Critch, but better late than never. Anyways I'm obliged to you for not tellin' the marshal that I stole that money off of you.'

'Quite all right,' Critch said easily. 'Think nothing of it.'

'O' course,' Arlie continued thoughtfully. 'I reckon *I* was kinda doin' you a favor by not tellin' him I stole it from you. The kinda money that was, it wasn't exactly comfortable t' have a claim on it.'

'But I did claim it, dear brother. I admitted that it was mine.'

'Uh-huh, sure. After you'd had time to think up a story to go with it.'

'Why don't we put it this way?' Critch said. 'You

don't owe me anything, and I don't owe you anything.'

Arlie hesitated; then, shook his head. Said he reckoned Critch did owe him something. 'Look how I spoke up for you when the marshal had you pinned for murderin' Big Sis! Claimed I done it myself, didn't I?'

'What about it?' Critch said. 'I did the same thing for you.'

'Yea, sure. Because you wanted to make yourself look good to Paw! I know, because I, uh – Anyways, you knew danged well you wasn't running any risk by confessing! What the hell? If Marshal Harry'd had any idea that either one of us killed that woman, he'd've arrested us right away instead o' standing around talkin' for an hour!'

The brothers stared at each other. A teasing smile played around Critch's lips, and Arlie slowly reddened.

'Like you was sayin', little brother,' he grinned sheepishly. 'You don't owe me nothin' and I don't owe you nothing. We was both tryin' to make up to Paw. We both knew we was safe confessin' t'the murder. Reckon we think so much alike that, uh . . .'

He broke off, giving his brother a long penetrating look. Then, asked if he could ask a fair question.

'By all means,' Critch said.

'Well, looky, then . . . how do you honest-to-God feel about me? I mean, do you ever sort of feel that you'd like to, uh, have this place to yourself? If you could work it out safe and easy, I mean.'

'I'll ask you a question,' Critch said. 'The same one.'

'Well, uh, would you believe me if I told you?'

'Would you believe *me* if I told you?' Critch asked.

Arlie scowled at him. Then, gradually, the scowl crinkled into a smile, and he burst into whoops of laughter.

'God damn, little brother! They's sure as hell one thing for sure!'

'Which is?'

'We may have to bust our ass on this place, but we sure ain't never gonna get bored! No, sir, they ain't never gonna be a dull minute for you an' me!'

Critch chuckled agreement.

As they rode on through the fall afternoon, Joshie and Kay, who had been primly decorous theretofore, were suddenly overcome with a spasm of giggling, the sound of which drifted up to the two men. Arlie tried to make his face severe – after all, he was the family's eldest now. Failing miserably in the attempt, he spoke chidingly to his brother.

The squaws were getting out of hand, he declared, and it was largely Critch's fault. For where you had one squaw with a man and one without, there was no damn telling what might happen. And what the by-God was wrong with Critch that he didn't marry Joshie?

'What's the hurry?' Critch shrugged. 'I'll get around to it some day.'

'*Some day?* What kind of answer is that? You like her don't you.'

'Very much. In fact, I think she's the most delightful female I've ever known.'

'Well, she's crazy about you, too. So marry her, dammit! She needs a man, and you need a woman.'

'Oh,' Critch said innocently. 'You mean we need each other to sleep with? That's why we should get married?'

219

Arlie said, why, sure, what else, adding that he had been greatly concerned about his brother's sexless state. 'It just ain't natural for a man not to be gettin' his stuff,' he said darkly. 'An' it sure don't do a squaw no good either. Why, it plumb makes me shiver t'think what might happen, if you an' Joshie don't start knockin' it off pretty soon. Might go crazy as bed bugs.'

'Well, gracious me!' Critch said. 'We certainly can't have that, now can we?'

He looked over his shoulder, swung an arm in a beckoning motion. The two girls immediately drew abreast of them, and Critch lifted Joshie from her saddle and onto his own.

She cuddled against him happily, giving him the reins of her horse. While Arlie stared dumbfounded, Critch suggested that his brother and Kay take a long ride by themselves, since he and Joshie had private business to transact at the hotel.

'We usually take care of it at bedtime,' he explained, 'but that suddenly seems too long to wait. I hope you don't mind . . . big brother?'

Arlie gulped; scowled. 'Now, looky here—' he began. 'What the hell's goin' on here? What kind of business you takin' care of, anyways?'

'Well . . .' Critch arched an amused brow at him. 'Let's just say that it isn't fiddling, but it's something that rhymes with the word.'

Joshie again burst into giggles, quivering deliciously against him. Kay gave Arlie a resigned look, then rolled her eyes heavenward.

'Ho, boy,' she sighed, 'you plenty damn stupid, ol' husband.'

'But – but – God dang it!' Arlie looked helplessly

from his wife to Critch and Joshie. 'I mean, why, hell's fire—!'

He blinked his eyes. Vigorously shook his head in the manner of a man recovering from a hard punch. Somehow, as Critch began to draw away with Joshie, he managed to raise his voice in a feeble facsimile of insouciance.

'Ride her easy, little brother! Take your spurs off before you mount!'

'Leave spurs on,' Kay called. 'Make ol' Joshie jump!'

'I jump anyway!' Joshie called back happily. 'Ol' Critch, he plenty damn man!'

THE END

WILD TOWN

by Jim Thompson

'My favourite crime novelist – often imitated but never duplicated – is Jim Thompson'
Stephen King

When David 'Bugs' McKenna is hired as the house detective for his hotel by Mike Hanlon, the town's crippled millionaire, McKenna has hopes that he can leave his violent past behind. But the death of Dudley, the hotel auditor, the disappearance of $5,000 and the unwanted attentions of Lou Ford, the town's deputy sheriff, and Joyce, Hanlon's beautiful, young wife, mean that McKenna is looking at more trouble than he can handle. And either a long, long stretch in the State Pen or a longer stay in the town cemetery . . .

'A blisteringly imaginative crime novelist . . . mesmeric abilities as a story teller . . . he outwrote James M. Cain at his most violent, amoral, terse and fastmoving . . . a classic American writer'
Kirkus Reviews

'Dashiell Hammett, Horace McCoy and Raymond Chandler . . . none of these men ever wrote a book within miles of Thompson's'
R.V. Cassil

0 552 13257 8

THE GETAWAY

by Jim Thompson

'Jim Thompson is the best suspense writer going, bar none'
New York Times

The bank robbery was a piece of cake. Everything went as smoothly as Doc McCoy had planned; they walked away with close on $300,000 and no one in pursuit. But that was when their problems began. For there was nothing easy or simple about the getaway.

'If Raymond Chandler, Dashiell Hammett and Cornell Woolrich could have joined together in some ungodly union and produced a literary offspring, Jim Thompson would be it'
Washington Post

'Read Jim Thompson and take a tour of hell'
The New Republic

0 552 13350 7

A SELECTED LIST OF CRIME NOVELS
AVAILABLE FROM CORGI BOOKS

THE PRICES SHOWN BELOW WERE CORRECT AT THE TIME OF GOING TO PRESS.
HOWEVER TRANSWORLD PUBLISHERS RESERVE THE RIGHT TO SHOW NEW
RETAIL PRICES ON COVERS WHICH MAY DIFFER FROM THOSE PREVIOUSLY
ADVERTISED IN THE TEXT OR ELSEWHERE.

All Corgi/Bantam Books are available at your bookshop or newsagent, or can be ordered from the following address:

Corgi/Bantam Books,
Cash Sales Department
P.O. Box 11, Falmouth, Cornwall TR10 9EN

Please send a cheque or postal order (no currency) and allow 60p for postage and packing for the first book plus 25p for the second book and 15p for each additional book ordered up to a maximum charge of £1.90 in UK.

B.F.P.O. customers please allow 60p for the first book, 25p for the second book plus 15p per copy for the next 7 books, thereafter 9p per book.

Overseas customers, including Eire, please allow £1.25 for postage and packing for the first book, 75p for the second book, and 28p for each subsequent title ordered.